The Visitor Series

The Visitor

Makes a Retreat

Book 1 by Julie B Cosgrove

Write Integrity Press

The Visitor Makes a Retreat
Copyright: ©2023 Julie B Cosgrove

ISBN: 978-1-951602-18-5

Published by Pursued Books: an imprint of

P Write Integrity Press
PO Box
Dallas, TX 75370

Printed in the United States of America.

Dedication

To those who struggle to forgive
the ones who wronged them.

Contents

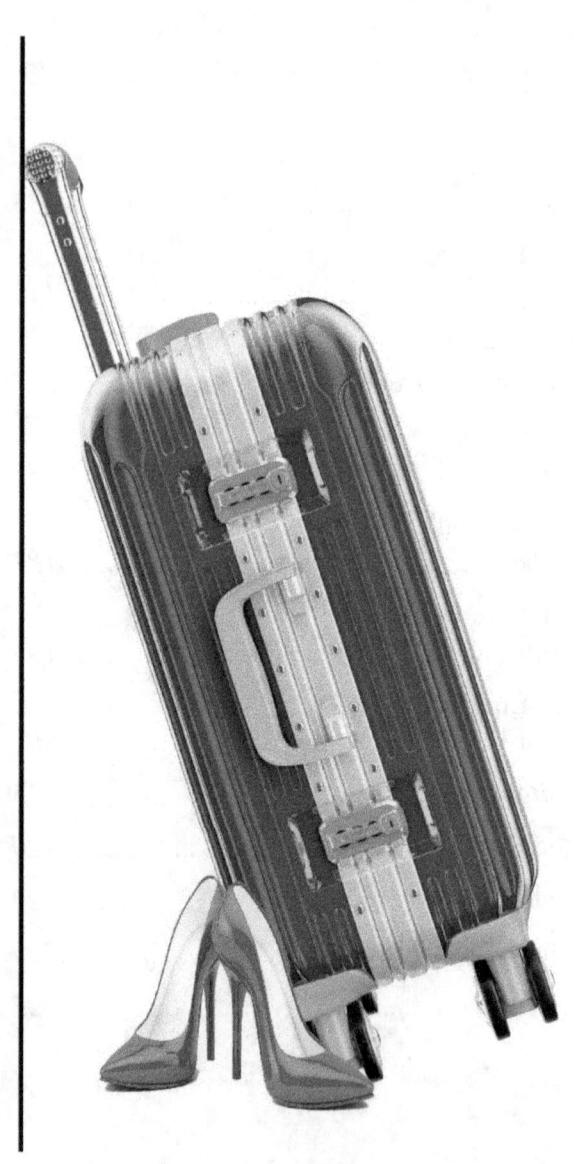

Chapter One

All Aboard

"*Mees* Fanny, your *sombrero*." Isabela Gutierrez hurried toward her employer with the broad-brimmed beach hat in her hands. She lowered her tone to barely above a whisper as she reached the woman. "I would hate for you to get sunburned." And in this part of Texas, it remained a possibility year-round.

"Thank you, Izzy." The dear elderly woman accepted it from her and plopped it securely on her head before wheeling her walker along the pavement toward the small group gathered at the bus.

Izzy watched as her employer played hostess,

smiling and flitting from guest to guest. Had she not still been using the walker after her hip displacement surgery, no one would have believed Fanny Henderson neared eighty years of age. But as her caregiver, Izzy knew just how exhausted the poor lady would be tonight after summoning all of her energy for today's trip.

Hopefully the weekend at the ranch wouldn't prove to be too taxing for her. In truth, though, Miss Fanny was only part of Izzy's concern.

Her boss had assured her that she would only act as her helper this weekend, and she wouldn't have to entertain. Hopefully, such would be the case.

A man passed her, bumping her shoulder slightly.

"Excuse me," she whispered to his back. He pulled his rolling case to the waiting bus and paused as he glanced, not at Izzy but at the elegant woman in red.

Connie Wright, Miss Fanny's niece and the CEO of The Wright Foundation that hosted this weekend's fundraiser, had arrived. She stepped next to her aunt and smiled at the couple beside her.

The man's gaze seemed to travel from Connie's lean, shapely legs all the way up.

Eww. It made Izzy want to take a shower, but Connie seemed to not notice.

Miss Fanny waved Izzy over. Carrying a check-in list on her clipboard, she rushed toward them as Miss Fanny introduced the couple to her niece.

"This is General and Mrs. Morton, my dear. General and Mrs. Morton, this is my niece, Connie Wright."

Izzy checked their names off the passenger list and watched Connie engage. The man's natural posture showed years of command. Chin up, shoulders straight. It made him observe everyone in a downward, almost condescending manner. But Connie spoke with an air of confidence that Izzy couldn't imagine having. The man even smiled at Connie at one point. His wife, Mrs. Morton, epitomized the stand-by-her-man military wife. Izzy noted she huddled in his shadow a lot yet exuded an aura of minor royalty.

Judging by their expressions, both appeared

utterly charmed by Connie Wright. After they stepped into the air-conditioned coach, Miss Fanny gestured in their direction. "He's retired Army and he knows his horses. His family bred two Derby winners. He is the sole heir of their fortune."

This fundraiser at the ranch should be perfect for him. Miss Fanny knew it, too, which is probably why she invited them to spend the weekend at the dude ranch in the Texas Hill Country. The Wright Foundation, famous for its support of children's charities, planned the event to introduce some philanthropic Houstonians to Equine Engages, a company that provided horse therapy. Miss Fanny, who knew everyone of influence in Houston, gladly offered to put the list of attendees together. Izzy suspected she'd do anything for her favorite niece.

A man with his cell phone glued to his ear approached Miss Fanny next.

"Mr. Roberts, I'd like to introduce you to my niece, Connie Wright of The Wright Foundation."

The man only nodded briefly in Connie's direction and then took the stairs onto the bus.

"What's his story?" Connie leaned toward

Miss Fanny and Izzy.

"Busy man. One of the richest attorneys in Houston, and he has a habit of making headlines."

He struck Izzy as a person of inflated self-importance.

Connie shrugged. "This type of thing wouldn't seem to be his vibe."

"You would think so, but he had a younger brother who suffered from spina bifida. He tends to have a soft spot for children's charities."

Her niece straightened. "My kind of guy."

Izzy stifled a giggle. She continued to check through her list as Miss Fanny made the introductions. Travis Thompson, who worked for TexLa Oil, and his wife Carolyn stepped up. Dr. and Mrs. Barker joined them. Connie had no problem including all four of them in her friendly banter.

How did she do that?

Elizabeth O'Connor joined the group. Izzy actually knew her. The daughter of a lifelong friend of Miss Fanny's, Elizabeth often visited her home in Houston. Close in age to the doctor and his wife she and Linda Barker began talking about some

social event that would occur next month. Miss
Fanny winked at Connie, then led the others onto
the bus.

Watson Banks, the man who had ogled
Connie, halted before boarding, took her hand, and
puckered his lips to kiss it. "Oh, dear no, Mr.
Banks." Connie chuckled and clasped his hand
instead. "This is Texas, not France."

"Indeed." He flashed her an innocent smile but
held onto Connie's hand until she politely slipped
it away.

Izzy tried not to shudder. The man just seemed
oily to her, but her mother had always told her that
the Good Book said not to judge. So, she placed
her concentration on the clipboard.

Shannon Lancaster came up at that point so
Izzy checked her off as the final name when Miss
Fanny introduced her. Mr. Banks barely looked in
Miss Lancaster's direction, but he seemed to hold
her complete attention.

"I'm not much of a horseman, Miss Wright. I
hope you'll assist me in that." He wiggled his
eyebrows at her.

"Oh, me neither." Miss Lancaster slipped her

hand around his elbow. "We can learn together."

He glanced down at her then with what Izzy interpreted as a rather confused smile. "Quite."

"You'll be in good hands. Both of you. The Circle C has a wonderful staff and just wait until you see the children." Connie began sharing the benefits of the charity they would be learning about.

Izzy compared the two women.

Connie, in a creamy lace blouse over a stylized rose-patterned sleeveless top and skinny jeans oozed confidence. Her deep red high heels accented the feeling and radiated professionalism.

Then Izzy glanced at Shannon, a pear-shaped woman in well-worn denim capris and a faded embroidered denim shirt. Her smile seemed genuine, though it showed an abundance of large, white teeth, but she had a soft demeanor about her. The type immediately attracted to puppies and babies.

"Ready to roll, Miss Henderson." The bus driver called in their direction.

Miss Fanny nodded at him. "Let's be off, then."

"Shall we, Miss Wright?" Watson Banks ignored the woman clinging to him and touched Connie's elbow.

Connie gave the man a small frown. "I'm sorry, I am driving my Aunt Fanny. She is much more comfortable riding in a car with her hip. You understand."

"Of course, she is, poor woman." Shannon gave a sympathetic shake of her head before she brightened. "I guess that just leaves the two of us?" She glanced expectantly at Mr. Banks.

"I suppose so." He glanced back at Connie before escorting the woman to the steps.

Izzy clamped her lips together against the smile that begged to come out. Instead, she fell into step behind Miss Fanny and Connie.

"You need to watch out for that man, Watson Banks. He's between marriages right now."

Connie took it in stride. "Not my type, Auntie."

"And what type is?" Miss Fanny gave her niece a sidelong glance.

"The strong, silent, absent type that I'll never meet." Connie laughed. "Besides, I get the impression that Shannon Lancaster is interested in the unattached Mr. Banks."

"Oh, that poor girl. A widow, you know." Izzy hovered, but her employer navigated the walker over a bumpy part of the asphalt, without any trouble. "Her husband created the machine that hollowed out cattle horns to make urns. Longhorn Legacies."

"I've heard of that company."

It sounded a little familiar to Izzy as well.

"Her husband's partner ended up patenting the machine in his own name and basically stealing the company out from under them. Her husband never recovered, emotionally or financially."

"And Shannon is on the list because?" Connie tilted her head.

Izzy had the same question. Everyone else had the money to support the charity.

"Her parents' land in south Texas just happens to be sitting on an underground lake of oil." She wiggled her eyebrow as she eased into the car.

"Ah," Connie shut her aunt's door and clicked the fob to open the trunk.

Izzy folded up the rollator and tucked it into

the storage unit between their suitcases. She climbed into the back passenger seat as Miss Fanny's window slid open.

"Are we ready to roll?"

Several inside the bus nodded and the bus driver shut the doors. A minute later the small convoy headed west.

It took an hour to crawl through the remainder of Houston traffic, but once at highway speed, Aunt Fanny quieted.

Izzy twisted to glance at her employer, who thankfully had fallen asleep. She leaned forward to whisper in Connie's ear. "If you need me to take over . . ."

Connie glanced at Izzy and the focused again on the bus in front of them. "Actually, I love to drive. It relaxes me, though I seldom get to drive my own car. Rentals mostly. Still, there is a certain freedom about it." Her chuckle sounded almost melodious. "Not as good as galloping over open fields bareback on a quarter horse, mind you."

Her comment surprised Izzy. "I thought you grew up in Chicago."

"Yes, in Mom and Dad's brownstone. I've

lived there all my life except for when I was in college, but I've never stayed there for long periods of time. It's a shame too. We're right in Lincoln Park with a view of Navy Pier on Lake Michigan from the balcony and of downtown if you peek through the other buildings. I live close to the zoo so sometimes in the early morning, if my windows are open, I hear the lions roar. Reminds me of the old MGM movies.

"But I love to ride." She brushed a few strands of dark brown hair off her face. "As a child, I'd visit Aunt Fanny and Uncle Lee on their ranch outside of Waco. Horses bonded us. Mom used to say my personality is a lot like Aunt Fanny's. We were both the youngest of our families. And we love horses."

"Sí. Your Aunt Fanny told me of her life with your uncle. How she sold everything and started over when he passed. Very sad."

"God has a way of planning our lives for the good. She dove into her career, kinda like me. Did you know she used to be a headhunter for some major corporations in Houston? Her degree in business with a minor in psychology helped her succeed. That is why I asked her to help me plan this event. Aunt Fanny knows everyone worth knowing in Houston. Plus, I haven't seen her in ages, so it gives us a chance to catch up."

"I recall seeing an old picture of your mother and Mees Fanny on her bureau."

Connie nodded. "Aunt Fanny is, I mean was, her youngest sibling. Mom was nine years older. She passed a few years ago, you know. Dad ten years before that, soon after they handed me the foundation to run." Her eyes lowered for a moment, almost as if she said a prayer in her parents' memory.

Izzy remained quiet out of respect.

After a moment, Connie continued. "I was an 'oops' baby. Mom was fifty. So, like Aunt Fanny, my siblings are quite a bit older, you see. I was homeschooled as I traveled with my parents around the country raising money for the foundation."

"Did that become lonely for you?"

"Oh, heavens, no. I met so many interesting folks. Besides, God blessed me with great parents who wanted to serve Him. They dedicated their lives to helping those of His children who need an extra bit of love and attention." A small sigh escaped from her lips. "They took Matthew 19:14 seriously. *'Let the little children come to Me, and do not forbid them; for of such is the kingdom of heaven.'* I do as well."

Then Connie's shoulders eased back against the car seat. "I guess because I learned the business from the get-go, I was destined to take over the foundation when they passed. All my other siblings had families, careers, even two of them had grandkids by then."

Her eyes traveled from the highway to the rearview mirror, then Izzy's face. Izzy noted a shimmer of emotion in them. This lady sure seemed to love her life and her family.

"Anyway, my aunt's ranch is where I learned to ride and fell in love with horses, so this charity is dear to my heart."

"Do you know any of the kids coming tomorrow?" Izzy didn't know much about the charity itself.

"No, but I know of them. Each is a precious, special case. The horses are trained to be gentle and patient. I have seen their videos. The change in the child after one ride is almost miraculous." She pointed up ahead with one finger while the rest remained wrapped around the steering wheel. "These folks in the bus? They are in for quite a treat."

Connie's infectious enthusiasm spread over Izzy. Even so, something in the back of Izzy's mind tickled as she watched the bus ahead, like the imaginary feather under one's nose that brings on the desire to scratch. Perhaps a nudge for her to be observant?

But then, when rich and powerful people rubbed elbows, there was always a chance for a few sparks. At the very least, she would keep an eye on that Watson fellow.

Chapter Two

Welcome Y'all

After a pleasant and surprisingly healthy lunch, Connie and Izzy browsed the gift shop while the Houstonians headed down Main Street in Fredericksburg to shop in the touristy section. Aunt Fanny snoozed on a comfy bench under a sprawling oak tree in the garden of the restaurant, restored from a Victorian home.

When they all boarded the bus, Izzy followed with her clipboard. Did she notice a bit of tension? The married couples sat in a group, chatting, except for the general who got out his pocketknife to clean his fingernails. Shannon sat across the aisle and joined in a conversation with Elizabeth.

Watson chose a seat on the opposite side and stared out the window. The attorney, still on his cell phone, perched in the very back near the onboard restroom, sprawling his boots over the entire row of seats. Several of the patrons sent the man disgusted eye-daggers—or did Izzy misinterpret their reactions?

Did they object to him conducting business, or whatever he did, instead of joining in the bonding session? Or did something else about him irritate their moods?

Pushing her observations to the back of her mind, she checked names off the list and counted heads. All present.

At four o'clock sharp, they rolled through the gates of the Circle C Dude Ranch. Bob and Margaret Blakely waved from the massive front porch that stretched across the main building. Wooden rocking chairs waited for tired travelers under softly whirring ceiling fans while urns of vincas and geraniums dotted the spaces in between the knotted cedar posts. A flank of steps, wide enough for four people to walk abreast, led to the double doors and lobby. Off to the left, an asphalt path led to a wooden ramp for the disabled near the end of the veranda. Izzy directed Miss Fanny and her walker in that way while the others followed the Blakely's into the building.

The newcomers moved to the main desk as Connie, who had held the door for her aunt, walked with Miss Fanny in that direction. Izzy glanced around with appreciation. The décor tastefully combined modern convenience with a western flair in a light, airy fashion. Even with the log cabin styled walls, nothing screamed overdone or cliché. No longhorns, branding irons, cowhide rugs, or dark crusty leather that loudly announced someone's sitting, thank goodness.

Izzy did notice an etching of a cowboy kneeling before a cross tastefully displayed on one wall, though. A Bible verse from second Chronicles about God's people praying for their land was etched into a plaque underneath it. Below that sat a chest-high bookcase filled with Bibles, DVDs and other books, some by Texan authors she'd read. On the wall over the check-in counter hung an iron cross with a circle around it.

Ah. Circle C. Izzy smiled.

Beyond the lobby lay two meeting rooms labeled the Bronc and the Stallion. On the other side sat a large dining room, named the Trough, and a lounge called the Paddock, which featured several conversational groupings. A double-sided river rock fireplace divided the two rooms. Wooden beams arched the highly pitched ceiling. Wagon wheels made into chandeliers added ambient lighting along with modern pod lights aimed at artwork by Hill Country artists, all on sale of course. Izzy glanced at a few of the prices and coughed into her fist, especially one by Jose Mendoza. Nice, colorful Texas flowers, but . . .

The couples dispersed and Connie brought over Izzy's room assignment. "It's really well done. Each of the rooms are named after types of horses." She handed the key to Izzy. "You and Aunt Fanny are assigned to the Paint, the one closest to the accessibility ramp."

"Thank you." Izzy gripped the key and moved to where Miss Fanny chatted with the general.

Izzy helped Miss Fanny maneuver to their cabin so she could freshen up. They returned less than an hour later. Connie waved to greet them.

She had changed for dinner into a calf-length denim skirt, a princess-seamed ruby blouse with slightly flared three-quarter length sleeves, and ruby colored high-heeled boots.

That lady truly had a special look. Izzy bet she could convey the same stately elegance in a t-shirt and tennis shoes.

The others promptly showed up for hors d'oeuvres, except Vernon Roberts who arrived ten minutes late, still on his cell phone.

As he passed through the room, Mrs. Barker stepped aside and sniffed in his direction. He didn't seem to notice. Mrs. Thompson openly glared at him, but he still appeared to be completely oblivious to how the guests moved apart, seemingly avoiding all contact with the man.

At dinner, served buffet style, the man seemed content to eat by himself, though Connie did sit briefly to chat with him before joining Miss Fanny. Who could tell what that was about, but she was the only person in the room, including Miss Fanny, who could seem to stomach the man's presence.

After dinner, the group met in the Stallion Room for the presentation Connie prepared.

"Ladies and gentlemen. I hope you are sufficiently sated from dinner."

While Connie entered into a polite discussion, Izzy glanced around. She resisted the temptation to clean up a dirty dish from the table behind her, then noticed Watson. He'd been sitting across from Shannon Lancaster. Watson moved over to a drink station, poured two cups of coffee, and then returned to his table. He offered one to Shannon with a flirty smile.

Wow. The man wasted no time, did he? Well, perhaps he only acted the gentleman. She shouldn't judge. And Shannon seemed pleased enough to accept the gesture. Giddy even.

The lights dimmed, and photos of children on horses, even teenagers, began to flick onto the screen.

Connie explained what they were seeing. "Equine therapy is not new, and this is a good thing because time has allowed extensive studies to confirm the amazing benefits this treatment has on the physically and mentally challenged. For amputees, straddling a horse helps improve their posture as well as tone their buttock, back and thigh muscles. Children with incapacitating injuries or physical challenges like spina bifida, muscular dystrophy, and skeletal birth defects show vast improvement in coordination, flexibility, and balance. The rhythmic movement of the horse is key in this process. The movement also brings a calmness to children with autism, Asperger's, attention deficit disorder and hyperactivity disorders."

As Connie continued, Izzy watched the patrons' faces and body language. Each seemed riveted to the presentation. She commanded the room with professional poise yet presented a passion that drew her audience in with trust. All except that attorney who again sat at the back and appeared more interested in his phone than anything else.

Why had he bothered to come at all?

After the discussion, Connie and Miss Fanny stayed behind speaking to the general and his wife. Izzy was free to enjoy the cool of the patio for a few minutes. Carolyn and Travis moved in her direction. Sure, she wore a dark jacket and jeans, but she hadn't thought she'd be invisible in the shadows there. But they sure didn't mind talking in front of her.

"I wish he'd leave." Travis had a hard tone to his voice. "I know it's been years but seeing that snake still makes my skin crawl."

"Darling, please don't let him give you heartburn. It makes you snore."

Oh, my. Surely they didn't realize Izzy stood there. She folded herself into the shadows and hoped they wouldn't notice her.

"Remember what our pastor said?" Carolyn's mention of their pastor brought a seriousness to the conversation. "Forgiveness sets us free more than the person who receives it."

"Yeah, well I can't forgive the man for what he did." He stomped ahead of her with his hands thrust into his pockets.

Izzy gulped and shifted her focus to Miss Fanny who now perched in the doorway.

"I heard. None of our business." Miss Fanny took one hand off her rollator long enough to brush their comments away like a horsefly buzzing her ear. "Attorneys do make enemies sometimes. It's the way of the corporate world, but these wheelers and dealers are usually friendly to each other in public. All we can do is pray they remain civil to one another over this weekend."

Even so, Izzy wondered what the man could have done to solicit such hatred.

The Visitor Makes a Retreat

Chapter Three

Discontent

Though she usually retired at nine-ish, tonight Izzy's client seemed more exhausted than normal. And rightly so, considering the way she'd practically danced around the room before dinner and then again after the presentation to speak to almost everyone in depth. "Do you want to turn in a bit early?"

"Yes, dear Izzy. My bones are aching."

After tucking in Miss Fanny for the night, Izzy grabbed the riveting suspense mystery by Marji Laine and sat on the private patio. She opened to her bookmark in *Counter Point,* relishing the cool night breeze that carried the soft chorus of a chuck's-will-widow, the Texas version of a nightingale.

Then a man and woman's voice floated from the patio next door. "I don't care if he gives this charity a million dollars," the man said. "Never should have been allowed on the bus. His money is tainted, I tell you. Stamped by the devil himself."

"Albert, hush. Others will hear you."

"You think I care? What he did to Anthony bordered on criminality. He paid off those jurors."

"Sweetheart, that was a long time ago. Remember your heart . . ." The woman with the distinctive whine to her voice had to be Brooke Morton.

"My heart is fine." The general practically spat out the words. "It's his that needs a stake driven through it."

Izzy set aside her book. A real-life drama displayed before her.

The general's voice boomed through the fence again. "Anthony and Betsy would still be married today, and their kids not half as messed up as they are if it hadn't been for that lawsuit. Trumped up evidence. Vernon's key witness lied through his teeth and never blinked."

"Albert, you don't know that."

"Yes, I do. And so, do you." A slammed door punctuated the conversation's abrupt end.

Izzy jolted, her hand to her heart. Sucking in a deep breath, she peered through a knothole. Brooke slumped into a chair. Izzy almost went over to console the poor woman, but Miss Fanny wouldn't have approved. This was none of Izzy's business and Mrs. Morton would probably be embarrassed that the tirade had been overheard.

Still, it seemed like several on this bus tour had a grudge against Vernon A. Roberts, Attorney at Law.

Izzy sat in silence absorbing the conversations she'd heard. Maybe Connie needed to be filled in. The growing animosity could affect the outcome of the whole event. Izzy called Connie on her cell. "Could we meet in private?"

"Sure. Meet me at the Canteen in five."

Izzy slipped the book into her coat pocket and walked over to the snack area by the pool that all the private porches accessed. She found a few dollars in her other pocket and bought herself a ginger ale from the vending machine. After a few minutes she heard Connie's light footfall. She had changed into a faded pair of jeans, a Chicago Cubs t-shirt, and well-worn sneakers. Izzy marveled that she still appeared polished.

"What's up?"

"I have overheard two conversations that I think you should know about."

"Oh?" Connie pulled up a chair.

Izzy glanced around and sat across from her. A man in an odd-shaped hat raked up clippings near the bushes at the edge of the pool, illuminated dimly by the lights under the water.

"I hope I won't bother you ladies." The gardener hunched over his rake but paused and touched the edge of his cap.

"No worries." Connie flashed him a smile and waved.

It seemed a strange time for him to be gardening, but clearly Connie wasn't bothered by him. Poor man must work long hours.

Izzy leaned over the small table to speak softly anyway. After she had relayed the two conversations as close to verbatim as she remembered, Connie sat back and stared out into the darkness for a moment. Then she scooted forward and laced her fingers together. "I know people in high societies, even in large cities, can run in small circles. Everyone knows the scoop on everyone else. In the past I've learned to keep everyone focused on the charity, not each other." She patted Izzy's hand. "It'll be fine, but I greatly appreciate you giving me a heads up."

Izzy felt her shoulders relax.

Connie snickered. "Between you and me and the trees, I came close to yanking that blasted phone from the man's hands, though. I mean, how rude."

Giving Izzy that charming wink of hers, Connie said good night and sauntered off to her cabin.

The breeze rustled through the oaks and played with the submerged lights of the pool. No sounds came from the cabins, and one by one, their lights went out. Izzy almost expected to hear "Good night, John Boy" filter over the peace of the countryside.

Chuckling to herself, she gulped the last of her

soda and yawned. Perhaps it all would blow over by morning. She wrapped her jacket closer around her and slipped back through the privacy gate to her suite.

When Izzy and Miss Fanny arrived at the Trough the next morning for breakfast, Connie and Elizabeth were already there. The rest of the group came trickling inside in small groups.

Izzy noticed that Watson's hair seemed damp, as if he'd just showered and rushed from his room. He followed Shannon to a table.

Three ladies, all in their mid-thirties if Izzy had been asked to guess, sat off to the corner, their plates piled from the buffet. They laughed and talked rather loudly. Sounded like a girls' weekend off.

But they weren't part of the charity fundraiser group, so they weren't her problem. She raised on tiptoes to count heads. Nine, plus her, Connie, and Miss Fanny. Someone dilly-dallied.

"Anything wrong?" Connie came to her side.

"No, just checking off who is here. We are missing . . . ah, our illustrious attorney. No doubt on an important call." She scoffed.

They shrugged in unison and joined the line to get breakfast from the vast selection.

Izzy had cleaned her plate and even imbibed in a second mini-blueberry muffin when she realized that Vernon Roberts still had not arrived. She mentioned as much to Miss Fanny.

"Maybe he isn't a breakfast eater?"

Mrs. Blakely overheard the conversation as she refilled Miss Fanny's coffee cup. "I served him chamomile tea and toast at the pool about six thirty this morning. When I got there, he was swimming laps, so I left them on the side table near his towel on the lounge chair. He waved and said thanks."

"See, that's probably all he eats." Connie let off a small sigh and took a bite of her quiche.

Izzy scrunched her eyebrows though her mother told her never to do that because it caused wrinkles.

Connie downed the rest of her food and then excused herself. She went from table to table to casually speak with each guest while they ate.

After making the rounds, she clapped her hands. "Okay, folks. Let's all meet at the stables at nine-thirty sharp. Thank you." She turned to Mrs. Blakely. "Would you mind ringing Mr. Roberts's cabin and telling him about the plan?"

The proprietor stated she would but as Connie and Izzy left with Miss Fanny, Mrs. Blakely's hurried footsteps sounded behind them. "Miss Wright. I phoned but no one answered."

"No worries."

Izzy pointed in the direction of Watson who walked ahead. "Isn't he Mr. Robert's roommate?"

Connie gave a quick nod and called to the man.

He stopped and swiveled around, a creepy smile easing across his lips.

Eww again.

Watson's leer faded into a scowl then he shook his head and walked on.

Connie returned to her and Miss Fanny. "Funny. He hasn't heard a peep from the man's bedroom. Though he recalls being awakened by the squeak of a privacy gate."

"Well, that's when he must have gone

swimming. Surely, he isn't still there." The man would be a prune at this point. And with his very fair skin, he'd be quite a rosy prune at that.

Miss Fanny waved her hand. "You two better go check. I'm fine."

Connie hesitated.

Izzy caught the elderly woman's gaze. "Are you sure?"

"I'm fine. I'm fine. Go find that horse's rear end and see if you two can charm some of the acid out of him."

They both chuckled.

If anyone could charm him, Miss Connie would. As long as Miss Fanny was sure about it, Izzy wanted to tag along, though she had no intention of actually speaking to the man. She couldn't put her finger on it, but there were inconsistencies about him. She followed Connie around the side to the canteen. There he lay on the lounge chair, snoozing.

She glanced at Connie who gave her an eye roll.

"I'll go." Connie went over to jostle him awake.

But when she bent down, her hand recoiled and went to her mouth. She stepped back so fast, she almost fell in the pool.

Izzy rushed to her. "What's . . .?" She stopped. "Oh, my."

Vernon Roberts lay with his eyes wide open, staring into space. His jaw hung loose, and his lips had a bluish tint.

"Is he breathing?" Connie fiddled with the collar of her blouse.

Izzy put her hand in front of the man's open mouth. "I think he is, but only barely."

Connie sucked in a breath and reached for his wrist, placing two fingers on it. Her eyes shifted to Izzy. "Faint pulse. Go get Dr. Barker. I'm calling 9-1-1."

Chapter Four

Horseplay?

Izzy moved aside when Dr. Barker and Bob Blakely arrived.

"We found him like this." Connie stood as Dr. Barker kneeled over the man and set a small backpack down. She glanced at Mr. Blakely. "Your wife had mentioned bringing him toast and tea out here this morning, so we came looking for him."

Izzy glanced at the empty table next to him. Had Margaret Blakely come back to fetch the empty dishes?

Everything began happening quickly at that point. Several members of the group and the trio of young women had followed the doctor out. They crowded this side of the pool deck like they were onlookers at a zoo.

Izzy had to concentrate on keeping her posture level. With so many people staring at her along with the doctor and Connie, she wanted to squeeze her shoulders up around her ears as though she could hide behind them.

Dr. Barker was able to revive Vernon enough that the man vomited on the pool deck. He still seemed terribly woozy, though. The small crowd backed away a bit at that point just as approaching sirens sounded in the distance.

Mr. Blakely reported that Vernon would be fine and to please disperse so the EMTs could do their jobs.

Izzy turned to go, happy to leave him to it, though most of the others huddled near the Canteen on the other side.

"Oh, no, Mrs. Gutierrez." Mr. Blakely touched Izzy's shoulder. "You need to stay. I'm sure the police will have some questions for you and Miss Wright."

The police had been called? Why?

The ambulance arrived minutes before the

Sandersons' trailers with the horses. Connie rushed to meet the Sandersons. Mr. Blakely lifted his hand as though to say something, but she was a quick one, even in her high-heeled boots.

The EMTs loaded Mr. Roberts onto a gurney and wheeled him around the side of the main building toward their waiting ambulance.

Dr. Barker stood up and heaved a sigh. Slowly the small crowd moved toward him like reporters at a scene of an accident, Mrs. Baker leading them.

"That was a close call alright." He nodded to her as she approached.

She laid her hand on his arm. "Will he be okay?"

"Did he have a heart attack?" Carolyn Thompson fiddled with the beads around her neck.

"He exhibited the symptoms. But he seemed more alert when they wheeled him into the ambulance." Dr. Barker rolled down his sleeves.

Izzy's heart settled a bit knowing the man didn't lie on death's door.

"A shame it wasn't more severe."

The hiss startled Izzy and she turned to find Shannon behind her.

"You don't mean that." Brooke Morton, with her soothing, calming voice, patted Shannon's hand.

But Shannon didn't back down. "He deserves whatever happens to him."

Her, too? How many people did this man tick off?

Izzy decided to keep her ears open and her mouth shut. After all, most of these wealthy people saw her as a servant to Miss Fanny trained to act as those in their employ would—an almost invisible non-entity who moved amongst them discreetly doing her duty, sworn to silence. And Izzy was good at the silence part. If anyone could glean information, she could.

Miss Fanny appeared at the edge of the pool deck. "Let's all meet down at the stables."

Well, the police hadn't shown up yet. There was no good reason to delay the festivities of the day. When they had all assembled at the stables, Connie acted as though nothing odd had just occurred. "We want you to get to know each of the horses. They have been specially trained to accommodate certain disabilities." She introduced

Judy and Zac Sanderson who owned Equine Engages, a special summer camp outside of Kerrville. "They open their camp on weekends for children in San Antonio and Austin who could not otherwise afford equine therapy."

Carolyn raised her hand. "So why bring us Houstonians out here?"

Connie's eyes gleamed. "Excellent point." She turned to the horsewoman. "Judy, why don't you answer her question."

The thirty-something slender woman in riding jeans stepped forward. "We have been blessed with a donation of fifty acres to the west of Sugarland on the Brazos River. But we need funds to renovate the house, barns, and other outbuildings, as well as purchase and train the horses." She reached into her canvas satchel with the company logo on it. "I have a preliminary survey and estimate of the cost if anyone would like to view it. We are in the process of obtaining the permits now and our contractors do not expect any glitches. We are planning the grand opening, God willing, next June."

Watson Banks, Carolyn Thompson, and Linda

Barker raised their hands to receive more information.

Izzy glanced at Connie and gave her a thumbs up.

Connie responded with a slight head bob then turned her attention to the others. "Now let's step back and let them unload the horses, tell us their names, and for which special needs they are trained."

The morning went well. Even General Morton had the horses eating out of his hand, literally. Elizabeth took a special shine to a brown and white paint named Charlie. "I used to wear that perfume in my younger days. My late husband's favorite."

Izzy leaned down to Miss Fanny seated on her rollator. "How did her husband die?"

"Suicide about fourteen years ago." Aunt Fanny matched Izzy's soft tone. "Something to do with a lawsuit over a popsicle whose stick had plastic loops. Victor designed it so that when joined together kids could make them into things, sort of like tinker toys. One kid got his tongue stuck in a loop and had to have part of it amputated. His parents got millions and bankrupted poor Victor's fledgling company. It had been his dream and he'd left a lucrative engineering job to start it."

Izzy felt a chill cascade down her arms. She wondered if Mr. Roberts had been the attorney. She recalled a coldness in Elizabeth's steel gray eyes as she watched the EMTs wheel the man inside the ambulance.

Speaking of which, Mrs. Blakely headed toward them. Her head lowered, she walked with her arms wrapped around her torso. Izzy shot a glance at Connie who excused herself from the group and met the dude ranch caretaker halfway. The two chatted for a few moments then headed back to the main house.

Izzy turned to Miss Fanny. "Wonder if it had anything to do with news on Mr. Vernon?"

Miss Fanny responded in her elderly wisdom. "We'll find out soon enough, right? No need fretting."

A cloud of dust appeared on the road leading from the cattle guard. A white vehicle with Kerr County Sheriff painted on its doors pulled up to the main house. Two men in tan shirts, black trousers, and Stetsons got out and walked inside. Then a van pulled up and more men climbed out, this time in white jumpsuits carrying black cases.

Murmurings erupted around Izzy. Clearly, she hadn't been the only one to notice the official activity.

Miss Fanny shushed the growing whispers. "Now folks. Let's keep our attention on the Sandersons and their lovely horses. You will each get a turn to ride them if you wish."

A few minutes later, Connie returned to the group. She leaned in and whispered in Miss Fanny's ear then stood erect. "Ladies and Gentlemen. Sheriff Tate has requested we gather in the Stallion meeting room. Please head that way now." She leaned toward Zac and Judy Sanderson and spoke low for a moment before joining the rest of them.

"Now, wait a minute. What is this all about?" General Morton halted at the front of the line.

"The sheriff will explain everything." Connie assured him. She dropped to the back, falling into step beside Izzy, and let her aunt take the lead with the Morton's.

"What's going on?" Izzy lightly covered her mouth so no one ahead of her could hear.

Connie slowed to a stop, watching the others as they continued along the road. Then she peered into Izzy's face. Her jaw twitched. "It appears that our illustrious attorney didn't have a heart attack, per se. His heartbeat slowed and his blood pressure plummeted. But he also showed signs of gastric distress. They found traces of oleander in his stomach."

Izzy thought of the ones planted around the pool area as a natural privacy fence. "Why would he eat leaves off of a flowering bush?"

Connie started walking again but kept her voice low. "I doubt he would. But plenty ended up in his system. Their guess is it had been brewed in his tea. Not enough to kill him, but sufficient to make him very sick. He'll be in the hospital at least two more days."

Izzy gasped. "You don't think anyone in the group did this, do you?"

"I'm afraid I had to tell the sheriff about the conversations you overheard. He didn't appear pleased. Let's pray all is much ado about nothing."

Izzy's head spun. This could completely sabotage the weekend retreat. Could the rest of them be in danger? Miss Fanny? Connie? Extra diligence would be required to protect them.

The sheriff nodded as they entered the meeting room. Izzy noticed him chewing on something. Ah, a toothpick. Perhaps the man had recently given up smoking. Then again, it seemed rather stereotypical, didn't it?

He cleared his throat to get everyone's attention. "Ladies and gentlemen. I have a report from the hospital on Mr. Vernon Roberts, who, I am told, was a member of your tour group."

"*Was?* Did he die?" Elizabeth's hand went to her mouth.

"The world is a better place." General Morton scoffed as he crossed his arms.

His wife scolded him in a little squeak and pawed his forearm.

Sheriff Tate sauntered over to him. "Interesting response. And you are?"

"Albert Morton, *General* Albert Morton, retired Army."

The sheriff glanced at a deputy behind him

who was scribbling on a digital notebook. Another deputy moved to block the main exit while a third stood near the door that led out to the patio.

Izzy's stomach twisted. Did they actually think one of them tried to kill Mr. Roberts?

The sheriff strutted back to the front of the room, his thumb in his belt near his revolver holster. "It appears Mr. Roberts has been poisoned."

Carolyn groaned.

Elizabeth whimpered. "Then he *is* dead."

Watson snorted.

Travis stood. "By what? Something he ate? Should we be concerned?" His fingers gripped his stomach.

The question stimulated a gasp from someone. Izzy twisted to notice Carolyn Thompson sit down hard on one of the sofas.

Miss Fanny joined her on the couch. She picked up a brochure from the table next to her and began fanning the other woman. "We're gonna be fine, dear. None of the rest of us are sick."

The sheriff held his hands palms up as if to quiet their fears. "Now folks. No need to get all riled up. Vernon Roberts is on a lengthy road to recovery, and I don't believe any of the rest of y'all are in danger."

"Well, that's a shame." The whispered response came from Watson Banks who stood behind Izzy. She slipped sideways away from him.

The sheriff continued, though. Apparently, he hadn't heard the remark. "But you will all need to remain here in the main building until you are dismissed. We'll be conducting short interviews in the next room and my team will be searching your cabins."

"You have no right." Travis Thompson wagged his finger.

"Sir, sit down, please." The sheriff eyed him until the man did. The other men in the room gravitated toward chairs as well.

Then he slipped off his Stetson and raked his fingers through his sweat-darkened blond hair and put the hat back on. "Mr. Blakely is the one who owns these cabins. He's given his permission. At this time, we won't be touching your personal possessions."

"At this time? What does that mean?" The

general's face reddened.

Elizabeth suddenly busied herself dusting her slacks.

Izzy noticed Watson Banks shift in his chair.

Shannon sniffed and glanced out the window.

Mrs. Blakely clutched at her husband's hand and dabbed her eyes with a tissue.

And Izzy herself suddenly felt as if she was in a whodunnit movie.

Cut. Script, please?

The Visitor Makes a Retreat

Chapter Five

The List Grows

After the sheriff left to set up the interview room, Izzy pulled Connie aside and told her what Aunt Fanny had divulged about Elizabeth's husband. "Do you think Vernon Roberts was one of the attorneys?"

"One way to find out." She pulled out her phone and did an internet search. "Victor O'Connor, correct?"

Izzy shrugged. "Sounds right. Miss Fanny said it happened about fourteen years ago."

"In Houston?"

"I guess you could start there."

Connie's thumbs flew over the miniature

buttons on the screen. "Here's his obituary."

"Is there anything about a court case?" Surely, she would find something. Izzy peered at the tiny screen over Connie's shoulder.

"Headline for the *Houston Chronicle*. 'Popsicle Kid's Parents Awarded Millions.'"

Izzy scanned the article from her vantage point.

"There." Connie snapped her fingers and pointed at the screen. Sure enough. "Prosecuting attorney team lead by Vernon A. Roberts."

Izzy stared at Connie and then jolted when the sheriff came back into the room.

Connie turned toward him. "Um, Sheriff Tate?"

He stopped at the door jamb and pivoted back.

She motioned him over and handed him her phone.

Izzy watched as his eyes traveled the page.

"Humph." He removed a well-chewed toothpick from the corner of his mouth and pointed it at her screen. "Thank you. Can you print that for me please?" He walked away before hearing her reply.

Connie exhaled through her nose. "I guess we'll try, huh? I'm sure our hosts have a printer." She walked toward the main office.

Izzy wandered over to Miss Fanny whose face appeared exceptionally pale. "Ma'am. Do you need to lie down?"

"No, dear. But this is very disconcerting indeed. My poor niece. She's put so much time and effort into this event."

"As have you." Izzy patted her hand. "Let me fetch you a cup of tea."

Aunt Fanny flashed her a startled expression, then a smile grew on her lips. "I think I'll pass. Thank you, dear."

"You don't think that I would . . ."

She grabbed Izzy's sleeve. "No, no. Of course not, Izzy. But while I'm not looking, someone else might slip something in it. Especially if they still have something on them that they shouldn't."

"I hadn't thought of that."

"Water will be fine. Things dissolve in hot liquids faster than cold."

"Yes ma'am." Izzy moved to the door, but a deputy stepped into the room and blocked her way.

"Albert Morton?" the man announced.

"That's *General* to you, son." He remained seated.

"Yes, sir." The deputy stepped toward him. "This way, please."

The Army officer harumphed and rose with purpose, knocking his chair to the floor, then stormed out ahead of the officer.

Brooke cast her eyes to the carpet, her teeth tucking a quivering lip. Did she think her husband guilty or just belligerent?

Izzy quietly followed them from the room and then veered toward the kitchen. *Thank you, God, that I never met Vernon Roberts before yesterday. What a horrible man. Please help him recover and may this experience help him realize what a pompous you-know-what he is and that he really needs You.*

She felt her cheeks warm. Maybe she should have left that part out about his personality.

One by one, the deputy called the rest of the attendees to be interrogated, some taking longer than others. Izzy brought back a half-dozen water bottles and set them on the center-most side-table.

The general, Connie, and Travis Thompson stayed in the other room for quite some time after the deputy called them in. Brooke and Carolyn finished more quickly. Did that mean something?

Connie obviously would take time because she had information to share about this motley group. Either they suspected Travis Thompson and Albert Morton more because of their comments or they simply verified their whereabouts with their wives and let them leave. Hard to say. Part of her wished she could shrink to the size of a fly and cling to one of the corners of the room next door.

When Connie emerged, Izzy caught her by the elbow. "What happened?"

"They wondered if someone might have a grudge against Equine Engages."

"You mean sabotage the fundraiser?"

Connie bobbed her head. "Possibly. They are looking at all angles. Come, I need to speak with my aunt."

But they didn't have a chance. The deputy called Miss Fanny and the sheriff spent over a half hour with her.

Izzy tapped her fingernails. Miss Fanny had

still been terribly tired from her hostess duties yesterday. And she still seemed rather pale even after drinking some water. "What could they be doing? Have they no consideration for her age or condition?"

Connie placed a gentle touch on her shoulder. "Aunt Fanny can handle her own. You know that. They probably have a bunch of questions since she put the guest list together. Besides, she has lived most of her adult life in Houston. She knows their backgrounds and social movements."

"I guess. Still, I am going to see if she needs anything. She is under my care."

Izzy walked to the deputy guarding the room and spoke with a low voice. "I must check on Mees Fanny. I am her caregiver."

He motioned for her to follow but stopped her before she entered the Bronco Room. Through the door she heard her client's voice, loud but shaky. "Now, young man, I mean no disrespect but if you are insinuating I somehow orchestrated this travesty then you can speak to my attorney. This isn't a replay of Agatha Christie's *Orient Express* for goodness' sake."

Izzy turned to the deputy. "She should not be agitated." Without waiting for his permission or assistance, she pushed through the door. She didn't care if they arrested her, but they would treat Miss Fanny with care.

Sheriff Tate rose and came over to her.

She swallowed hard but pushed through her initial desire to turn and rush back to the silence of the other room. "Sheriff, you must realize that Mees Fanny is fragile."

"I'm not a piece of crystal, Izzy." She didn't sound nearly as strong as the words did and her voice had a little shake to it.

Izzy chose to ignore her employer. "She is recuperating, and this weekend is the first out of her home in months. She is not as healthy as she would like to believe." She didn't take her eyes off of the sheriff, but she could feel a piercing gaze from Miss Fanny. "I insist that you release her to her cabin for a rest. You can recall her after she has time to re . . . re-strengthen herself." That wasn't the right word. It probably wasn't a word at all, but it would get the point across.

As much as she wanted to look at the floor and

await the man's response, she kept her gaze locked with his.

He had listened with a marbled face.

After a standoff that lasted about three seconds, he switched his weight to his left foot and rubbed his chin. "Ma'am, I fully understand your concern. But we have to treat everyone equally."

"And yet, everyone is not equal, sir. It would be tragic if Mees Fanny had to be re-strengthened at the hospital because you distressed her too greatly." Again, it wasn't the right word, but it had worked the first time. His eyes narrowed as he seemed to consider her request. Then he glanced at Miss Fanny. The woman had propped her elbow onto the arm of a wingback chair and lightly rubbed her forehead with her eyes closed.

The sheriff sighed and nodded at Izzy. "I might need to speak with her again."

"Understood." It left her lips a whisper, but Izzy could have whooped with delight. "I will take her to her cabin to lie down."

"And then you'll return." It wasn't a question.

Izzy moved to Miss Fanny but glanced back at him and nodded. "Help me here." She motioned to the deputy who stood near the door. Between the two of them, they transferred Miss Fanny to sit on the bench of her rollator. Izzy then pushed her out of the room.

Miss Fanny turned her head and spoke over her shoulder. "That was pretty brave of you, my dear."

Hmm. It sort of was a little on the brave side, wasn't it?

Chapter Six

Gumption

It took the sheriff's team hours to interview everyone and to do a preliminary search of their kitchenettes. Izzy's name was the last to be called.

Just as lunch arrived, of course.

She moved toward the Bronco room, reminding herself that these men weren't her enemies even though the sheriff pushed Miss Fanny too far. Whoever did this to Vernon Roberts, on the other hand . . .

She sat and crossed her ankles, glancing at the floor. "I apologize for my outburst earlier."

"That was an outburst?" He actually smiled. "Don't think another thing about it, Mrs. Gutierrez.

I get tunnel vision with situations like this. And she is blessed to have you as a caregiver. My own mother-in-law suffered a stroke, and my wife had a dickens of a time finding someone she felt comfortable about caring for her."

Had he said blessed? Izzy's stomach muscles eased. Might she be sitting across from a believer? "Thank you."

"Now if I'm not mistaken by the clinking of silverware I heard as you came in, they're serving lunch?"

Then he called a deputy over. "Amos, go get a plate of food and iced tea for Mrs. Gutierrez, please?" He turned to Izzy. "Sweet?"

He ordered lunch for her? She gave a nod. The man was kinder than she'd given him credit for.

He stayed quiet until after the deputy exited and closed the door. "Now, according to Miss Wright, you overheard several of the guests complaining about Vernon Roberts's presence on this retreat."

"Yes." There was no need for her to explain how most people don't normally notice workers.

"I see. Tell me as close as you recall exactly

what each stated."

Despite his kind gesture, Izzy's heart still thumped against her blouse. She hated to be the center of attention, but she didn't need the sheriff thinking her nervousness meant she hid something. So, Izzy took a deep breath and silently sent up a quick prayer for courage.

She started with the General and then the Thompsons. By the time she got to Elizabeth, her food had arrived on a tray.

The sheriff waited while the man he'd called Amos set the tray down in front of her. "Thanks. See if you can scare up a glass of tea for me as well."

Izzy took a nibble of the barbeque brisket on a whole wheat bun. A bit spicy but not bad. Rich flavor. She swallowed then shared what she and Connie discovered about Victor O'Connor fourteen years ago in case the sheriff hadn't gotten the printout.

He nodded. "I got that from Miss Wright. Take a breather and go ahead and eat."

He pulled out a small notepad. "Your cabin is next to the duplex shared by the Morton's and the

Thompsons'. Then comes a cabin with Elizabeth O'Connor and Connie Wright and beyond them another one with Watson Bank and Vernon Roberts, correct?"

"Sí. That seems correct." She set the remains of her sandwich down and wiped her hands on the napkin. Placing it back on the tray, she picked up her glass of tea and sat back in her chair.

"Who decided who would be with whom?"

"The Blakelys assigned the cabins. I simply emailed them the list of guests. Of course, I requested that I share a cabin with Mees Fanny."

"How many did your employer invite?"

"I know she contacted over fifty people. She targeted those who had either an interest in horses or children with physical or emotional impairments."

He jotted something in his notebook and then glanced back up at her. "Are you an early riser?"

"Generally." What did that have to do with anything? "My goal is always to do whatever is needed to make Mees Fanny feel ready to meet the day."

The sheriff's right eyebrow cocked. "If you

ever want to move to the Hill Country let me know. My wife would be relieved to have someone like you caring for her maw."

Izzy blew out a puff of air at the notion. "You are very kind, but I could not consider leaving Mees Fanny."

"Did you do your Bible time this morning outside by some chance?"

Now how did he know she was a believer? "How did you . . ."

He held up a hand. "Your employer thinks quite highly of you."

Ah, of course. Miss Fanny never hid her beliefs. Sharing her thoughts about her relationship with the Lord might just intrigue someone else enough to want to know more about Him—as she put it. Though Izzy would have a hard time sharing something so deeply personal.

She took a breath and glanced downward for a moment. "As a matter of fact, I sat on the patio."

He bobbed his head several times. "What time?"

"About six-fifteen. Someone was in the pool, though I only heard the light splashing. I recall feeling that I should exercise in the morning like that. I thought it might be the general."

"Why?"

"Well . . ." Why *had* she thought that? "It was chilly. The water would be cold. I thought, since he was military, he might have a practice of exercise. Those in the military stay fit, do they not? Years of discipline and rigorous schedules."

He flashed her a small smile. If he had interviewed the others with this demeanor, she felt better about the whole ordeal.

"Can you recall anything else?"

Izzy felt a chill scoot across her forehead. Her mouth dropped open for a moment as her eyes widened. "Why, yes." Why had she not thought of that before?

The sheriff leaned forward and tilted his head as he opened his tablet.

"I overheard Mrs. Blakely call to Mr. Roberts that his tea and toast were on the table. That reminded me to go inside to start preparing tea for Mees Fanny."

He wrote it down. "So, after that you busied yourself with caring for your client."

"Sí, until we left for breakfast."

"Very well. Thank you."

Was that all? It hadn't gone half as bad as she imagined. She rose, set her glass on her tray, and lifted it as she made her way to the door.

The sheriff twisted toward the door as she passed. One of the men in white jump-suits came in. "Sir, we found something. In the Appaloosa. A pot used to boil water. Used today. There appears to be residue in the bottom."

"Get it to the lab, Jake."

Connie and Elizabeth's cabin. Izzy almost dropped her tray.

"There is more, sir. In the Palomino we found a small baggie of dried crushed leaves in a jar on the counter. Kinda looks like weed. But we aren't sure. I'll send that along as well."

The Barkers cabin. Now what would one of them be doing with that?

Izzy skittered into the other room and set her tray down next to Connie and Miss Fanny. She whispered. "I overheard one of the investigators tell the sheriff that they found a baggie like marijuana in the Barker's cabin."

Miss Fanny sighed. "Of course, they did. Carolyn Barker has suffered from fibromyalgia for decades. It medicinal, or so she says. Her husband is an orthopedist after all. I'm sure he prescribes it for her."

Watson Banks leaned closer to their table. "Helps with nausea from chemo as well."

Izzy hadn't realized the man had been eavesdropping. Good thing she hadn't shared the rest of what she had learned.

He continued, "My first wife used it when her cancer returned. And also, near the end for the horrific pain." His eyes moistened.

"I'm so sorry, Mr. Banks. How tough that must have been for you." Connie gave him a soft smile which made his eyes brighten.

"Did it not make her high?" Izzy lifted her eyebrows. She knew very little of such things. Connie eyed her over the rim of her iced tea glass. "Not if brewed from the dried flowers. Or if it first undergoes what is called decarboxylation to release the chemical that makes people's brains react funny."

Miss Fanny coughed. "Dear niece, I am an old

woman and very little surprises me anymore. However, I am shocked you know such things."

"One of our charities works with children who suffer from certain disorders. They're doing a study of the effects of cannabis on children with epilepsy and MS. I attended a seminar on it last month as a matter of fact."

Miss Fanny nodded and proceeded to finish her lunch then excused herself. "You two stay here. I am just going to rest my eyes for a few minutes."

The two watched her leave then ate the remainder of their meal in silence. Something Connie mentioned didn't sit quite right with Izzy. She couldn't quite place a finger on it, though.

The deputy named Amos strode casually into the room and moved toward Elizabeth. He spoke to her, and the woman jerked toward him. As her face paled, she rose quietly and almost tiptoed from the room.

The deputy paused and turned to face the room. With a pleasant look on his face, he lifted his palms wide toward the group. "The rest of you may return to your afternoon activities, except for Dr. Barker." He put his palms together and gestured in the man's direction. "Sir, can you wait here? The sheriff has a few more questions of a professional nature."

"Of course." He fidgeted and tugged at his knitted shirt collar.

The rest began to rise from their seats. The deputy raised his voice over the crescendo of chatter. "We are asking that none of you leave this ranch until further notice."

"And when will that be, young man?" Albert Morton harrumphed.

"When we are finished with this investigation." He nodded and turned to go.

"So, you believe it to be an attempted murder?" Travis's voice cracked a little, but it was rather on the high side anyway so most likely nobody else noticed.

The deputy paused and glanced back at the man. "We don't discuss open investigations, sir." Then he continued back out into the hall.

Investigation. Of course, they'd been doing that all afternoon, but the deputy made it sound so official. So formal.

"This is ridiculous." The general practically

spat the words as he passed by the table where Izzy and Connie sat.

Watson glared at Travis for a moment. "A shame it was only attempted." His whisper was almost soundless.

Almost.

Izzy gave Connie a worried look.

"This will all blow over." Connie nodded. "You will see."

Izzy bobbed her head. And she would help it blow over quickly, if she could. Maybe Connie with her internet ability would help her.

And Watson Banks seemed to be the best person to start with, considering the comment she'd just heard.

He seemed a decent, down to earth man despite his wandering eye. And a question here or there shouldn't tear down any bridges. If she could force them out of her mouth.

But then, Miss Fanny had called her brave. She hurried to her cabin to awaken her patient, but Miss Fanny was already up and out, joining the group that had turned toward the arena. She walked fairly easily now and chatted with Elizabeth.

Clearly, her charge didn't need her. And it was easy to spot Watson Banks in the group. He trotted behind Connie like a puppy on an invisible leash.

Izzy charged ahead and caught up with him. She called out in a voice far too loud for her to normally use. "Mr. Banks."

The man halted and turned to face her.

Her throat tightened like it always did when her nerves tried to take over. She forced a swallow and took a breath. "Forgive me for intruding, but what type of cancer did your wife have?"

The amiable expression he held faded and he straightened to his full height. "Ovarian, why?"

"Well, it still seems to upset you." She hadn't really thought this through, but the words of her employer seem to come out of her mouth. "And I wondered if I could pray for you?" Wow. That wasn't at all what she'd expected to say. But it had come out much easier than she thought it would.

He scoffed and resumed walking. "I don't need prayer. I need justice. She didn't get it. Not in the least." He almost spat the statement out of his mouth as if the thought tasted bad.

She kept pace, not wishing to give up. "How

hard that must have been for you. I am sorry."

He surprised her when he suddenly took her by the elbow and pulled her to the edge of the road that led to the stable and stopped. "You seem genuinely interested so I'll explain. The doctor misdiagnosed her and several other women as well. Gave them hysterectomies but left the ovaries so they didn't have to go on hormones. Trouble being, that's where her cancer first formed, not in her uterus." He glanced toward the rest of the group. "I know you're a caregiver, so I gather you have medical training, and I'm not embarrassing you by discussing the particulars."

"Not at all." Truth was, talking with the man at all had her on the edge of a precipice. The topic had nothing to do with it.

Watson nodded and took in a deep breath through his nose. "After the surgery, she would still get these awful pains. The doctor kept telling her it was an ovarian cyst, that women got them now and again, and it would subside after a few months. By the time another doctor agreed to examine her, the cancer had spread up her spine to her brain."

"Oh dear." How horrid that must have been for both of them.

He pointed to his cabin. "And they had the audacity to put me in there with the shyster who defended the doc and got him off scot-free." His face reddened and the anger in his eyes made Izzy take a step back.

His focus sharpened. "Look, you seem like a nice lady. But if you really want to pray, thank God for me."

"For?"

"It took everything inside me not to suffocate the weasel in his sleep last night with my pillow. Tossed and turned, even paced the floor. Maybe God's removed the temptation from me, huh? At least I can sleep well tonight."

Watson kicked the ground and strode away.

Chapter Seven

Could it Be?

Izzy stood there a minute, torn between helping Miss Fanny to the stables or rushing back to tell the sheriff about her conversation with Watson. Then she saw the elderly woman stumble as a wheel jiggled over some gravel. Izzy dashed to her aid.

"I'm okay. A small rock hit my left wheel and it veered off, jerking one handle from my hand. That's all."

"Why don't you sit on the bench part, and I'll push you?"

"Well, that is something I will take you up on, if you think you can maneuver over this path. All this drama has worn me out." She nodded up ahead. "Connie seems to be all business though. She may just save this retreat after all. Here comes the bus of kids."

Childish laughter escaped from the bus's lowered windows. Several of the patrons turned to watch. Izzy could detect their moods had lightened as well by the smiles growing on their faces.

The bus pulled up next to the corral and stopped with a hiss of brakes. The Sandersons and Connie scurried to greet them as the front double-door swung open.

Izzy gulped as she saw the small bodies emerge with their nurses. One waddled with metal crutches clamped to her elbows. Two were carried down in wheelchairs, one with a metal halo around his head and screws in his skull. A Down Syndrome child showed such an innocent smile it touched Izzy's heart. Three more kids deboarded on their own, but one ran ahead and had to be corralled as he spun in a dervish fit with his arms out.

The rest of the adults held back, sensing the caretakers needed to manage the kids who had been transported by bus. But the smiles grew as some of the children were introduced and responded to the group.

If the grins and laughter were any indication, Miss Fanny was absolutely right in how this fundraising retreat would end up being successful.

Not all the adults were smiling, though. Elizabeth stood apart from the others—her face a blank.

Izzy casually wandered toward her. "Are you all right?"

"Fine." Her tone of voice didn't sound fine, though. "They do their research, I'll say that. They asked me all about Victor." She glanced at the barn and swallowed. "My husband. He committed suicide after a lawsuit bankrupted his company."

"I know. Mees Fanny told me. He seemed like a brilliant and caring man." Then Izzy realized Elizabeth might connect the dots and discover Izzy told the sheriff. She held her tongue in her teeth.

If the woman did make the connection, she didn't mention it. Instead, she just nodded and dabbed her eyes.

"He loved children, and we could never have any. His dream was to invent something fun and educational for them to do with plastic popsicle and ice cream sticks instead of them ending up in landfills and ocean bottoms." Suddenly, she turned her gaze toward Izzy and a fire flashed in her eyes. "They had the audacity of accusing me of poisoning that attorney. Just because I boil oregano tea for my IBS. Of all the nerve."

She then glanced down as if embarrassed she'd revealed too much and walked over to the rest of the group, leaving Izzy to mull over their conversation alone.

That's when what Connie said at lunch connected with her brain. Tea. Connie had talked about cannabis tea. Now how did she know Linda Barker consumed it that way? Unless, she had studied teas brewed with different plants and herbs. Maybe seeing Elizabeth brew her oregano tea gave her the idea of oleander tea.

Yes, Connie Wright had a fierce determination in her spirit. Izzy could tell the woman wielded power and enjoyed it. Brilliant strategist as well. Fervent for her foundation and its charities. A legacy she felt a deep obligation to carry on in her parents' memories.

And she had been to that conference. Learned about cannabis tea brewing. Maybe that's what gave her the idea. She told Miss Fanny about her interests in herbs. Did she know oleander could cause heart issues?

Did Vernon Roberts tell her to make certain he got his chamomile tea and toast at six-thirty sharp? Perhaps she'd overheard Vernon Roberts requesting an early morning snack. Would she dare put something in it to ensure he no longer tainted her efforts to raise money for this charity?

Her irritated voice replayed in Izzy's mind. *I felt like yanking his phone from his hand. How rude.*

Izzy's thoughts went a step further. Connie and Elizabeth did have a cabin next to Mr. Roberts. What if she boiled the oleander in Elizabeth's pot used for her oregano tea? Is that why they questioned the poor woman again?

It would be a smart move in order to divert attention from herself. But to implicate her aunt's dear friend in the process? Surely not.

Oh, dear. How could she think such a thing? Izzy's knees lost strength. She leaned against a corral post.

She had to admit the possibility did exist. However, such an action by Connie Wright could not only give the belligerent attorney cardiac symptoms, it would also break Miss Fanny's heart if she found out.

Chapter Eight

Horsing Around

Izzy's brain swirled so furiously it gave her a headache. When Aunt Fanny asked her to go get her wide-brimmed hat from the cabin to keep the sun off her head, Izzy gladly dashed away.

She sat on Miss Fanny's bed and sniffled. Her brain kept telling her what she'd thought made sense, but her heart remained conflicted. How could she think a thing of this kind visitor that her client loved so dearly? It gave her a twinge of guilt.

If only the pieces didn't fit so neatly.

She'd keep praying on it. And she wouldn't tell the sheriff. Not yet anyway. It might turn suspicion onto Miss Fanny as well. Speaking of . . .

As she grabbed the floppy beach hat from the closet, she heard a squeal out by the pool. Now what?

Izzy dashed through the privacy gate to find the three women from breakfast splashing each other in the pool.

One swam over to her. "We're sorry. Did we disturb your nap?"

"Huh? Oh, no. I just heard a scream and thought someone might need help."

The woman blushed. "No. Not at all. We were just horsing around." Then she covered her mouth and giggled. "Sorry. Being we are on a dude ranch. Didn't mean to make a pun."

Izzy giggled, too. And that felt wonderful.

The woman hung onto the side of the pool. "I'm Sally O'Brien. That's Ramona Redding in pink and Janice Lewis in gold."

They wiggled brightly manicured fingernails in greeting. Izzy waved back, realizing how short and stubby hers appeared.

"Girls' weekend," Janice called and then stretched out on her back in the pool. Her long blond hair looked like whitish-gold flames around her face.

Sally hopped up onto the nearby pool's edge and wrung out her hair. "And you are?"

"Izzy." She nodded. "I'm with The Wright Foundation retreat."

"Oh, the big group. Well, we were sorority sisters back in the day."

"After my time as a Dallas Cowboy cheerleader." Ramona lifted her chin.

"Seriously?" Janice splashed her. "Deary that's not nearly as impressive as your anti-wrinkle cream."

As though any of these young ladies dealt with wrinkles. Izzy resisted the urge to wipe her forehead.

Sally nodded. "She's right, though. Romana's Rose Cream. You should try it." She stopped and put her hand to her cheek. "Oh, I didn't mean you needed it."

"That's all right." The girl's openness was disarming.

"Well, it really is wonderful." She pointed at the blond. "And Janice is high up in Black Gold Enterprises."

Ramona cupped her palm to her mouth as though she was whispering, but practically shouted from the other side of the pool. "Oil, you know. Inherited oodles of it."

Janice splashed her again.

Sally shrugged. "I'm just a paralegal, but with my dad as the boss, I do pretty good. So, what do you do?"

"I'm the fulltime nurse for Miss Fanny Lee Henderson of Houston." Izzy heard the pride in her response, but she couldn't help it. She served a fine, genteel lady.

"I thought that was her. My mama knows her. Maybe I'll drop by later to say hi. We are staying over there until tomorrow afternoon." She pointed to a large cabin next to the canteen on the other side of the pool. "Then it's back to the grind on Monday."

"I'm glad you have this time together." Izzy held up the hat. "Duty calls."

"Okay. See you at dinner. Tootles." Sally slid back into the water and swam to huddle with her friends.

Izzy shook her head and walked back through

the patio, making sure she latched the gate. As she did another shriek echoed from the pool area followed by laughter. At least they had fun. No sheriffs or room searches to dampen their spirits.

She found the patrons and the children inside the corral. The Sandersons were demonstrating the bonding between the horses and the children. One boy brushed a brown mare down and readied to saddle it. He appeared to be maybe ten or eleven but handled the saddle well. Izzy noticed it was an English style instead of a western one, which amazed her. She handed the hat to Miss Fanny and leaned down to whisper to her. "Why are they on English saddles?"

"Why don't you ask?" Miss Fanny matched her whisper.

"Oh, I couldn't." Izzy wasn't a patron by any means. She didn't want to waste time away from those who were hopefully pledging money to the project, but her curiosity would not be quelled.

The older woman turned to face her with her eyebrow cocked.

Izzy raised her hand.

"Yes ma'am?" Judy lifted her gaze to Izzy.

"Why English saddles instead of the more common western ones?" Had that been too loud? Maybe sounded obnoxious?

"Great question." Judy patted one of the horses' necks.

Her accolade encouraged Izzy.

She glanced back at Izzy. "The English saddle gives the children's leg muscles more contact with the animal and the posting, which is the up and down movement as the horse trots, allows them to develop stronger back and buttocks muscles."

Several of the kids giggled when she said the word buttocks.

Izzy got lost in their joy and put all her speculations and worries to the back of her mind. Why, even the gruff general seemed to be smiling as he watched the children interact with the gentle beasts.

A glance to Connie as she leaned against the gate with her hands crossed over her waist told Izzy that she, too, was pleased, and perhaps relieved, that the events of the morning had not hampered this demonstration after all.

"Any of you folks want to ride, too?" Mr. and

Mrs. Blakely arrived with four saddled and reined horses in tow. "I know you didn't have an opportunity this morning."

They brought a black gelding with a white teardrop on his muzzle over to Connie and held out the reins.

"For me?" Connie's face lit as she squished the helmet over her bun and then hoisted a long, skinny-jean leg over the saddle. She moved away from the children and clicked her teeth. The animal transitioned to an easy trot and then a lope around the wide side of the large arena. Connie guided him toward a low obstacle and the horse had no trouble hopping over. Connie hardly moved.

"Oh." Shannon cried out, and many of the children responded as they would if they'd been watching fireworks.

Connie aimed for the medium obstacle that took a little more work, but the horse cleared it easily.

A couple of the children standing around the outer edge of the corral clapped their hands.

Mrs. Sanderson, called out. "There you go."

Connie did another loop and aimed for the

highest bar, a double.

"Oh, my." Izzy's heart pounded as the horse's gait accelerated.

He poised and leaped. Connie matched his movements perfectly as he landed on the other side and then slowed to an easy trot again.

The children cheered, many of the adults joined them. Watson Banks let out a loud whistle.

Miss Fanny pumped her clasped hands. "That's my girl."

Connie dismounted and handed the reins back to Mrs. Sanderson. "Oh, thank you. That felt so good." She grinned at her aunt and pulled off the helmet. "Been a while."

Elizabeth mounted the gelding at that point and trotted around the ring.

"Reminds me of old times back at the ranch. Oh, that I could ride like that now." Miss Fanny let out a long, nostalgic sigh.

Judy Sanderson overheard. "Why can't you? Come on. I can't think of a better demonstration for your guests."

"Really?" Miss Fanny's expression epitomized a child's face on Christmas morning.

Judy bobbed her head and helped her over to another horse. On command, the animal bowed close to the ground so Judy could maneuver the elderly lady's leg over the saddle and help her slip her feet in the stirrups as she sat down. Zac handed Miss Fanny the reins and patted the horse. "Up, Scout."

The majestic animal rose, almost in slow motion. Miss Fanny grinned from ear to ear as Judy guided the horse around the ring. Then she let Miss Fanny try a few turns on her own.

Everyone clapped.

Izzy felt warm tears trickle down her own cheeks. *Thank you, Lord for this wonderful moment after such a hard day.*

The children and horses from Equine Engage left a couple of hours later.

As she helped Miss Fanny walk back to her cabin to freshen for appetizers before dinner, Izzy noticed the forensic van had left but the sheriff's cruiser was still parked at the entrance. Funny, Dr.

Barker had never joined them. She hadn't even thought about it until now.

Again, the dilemma over speaking with Sheriff Tate about Connie's conversation needled her. Connie's and Miss Fanny's faces still showed the glow of their rides. Connie bent to kiss her aunt's cheek and then waved as she and Elizabeth left for their cabins.

"I'm going to take another little nap." Miss Fanny pushed the walker up the ramp and paused on the porch, glancing back at Izzy. "All that exhilaration has drained me. Think I'll skip the appetizer social. Will you let Connie know and then wake me in a bit?"

"Yes, ma'am." Izzy stood on the porch and glanced again at Connie, chatting with Elizabeth.

Izzy detected no deviousness about her. Sure, the woman had been raised to fundraise, but she also had a spirit of honesty and true commitment to her causes. No, Connie Wright may be a determined and powerful businesswoman, but she could never be a ruthless person.

Izzy went inside her cabin and sat on the sofa, staring out the window at the stables. Though the temperatures had only hovered in the high eighties today, the air conditioning felt wonderful.

Miss Fanny's soft snores already filtered through her partially closed door. Poor woman, such a trooper. She must be totally drained after all that had gone on this weekend, good and bad.

Izzy grabbed a throw pillow and hugged it to her, her mind wandering back to this retreat group.

Someone had been calloused enough to poison the attorney. Had they meant to kill Vernon Roberts and misjudged the dosage, or did they intentionally sicken him? Who would know about oleanders? Did any of them garden? Not likely. They all probably hired people for lawncare.

She guessed anyone could look these things up on the internet. The doctor obviously had researched about herbs and plants as well as prescription drugs. He did know oleander had that digi-thing in it. And he knew enough to prescribe marijuana for his wife's chronic pain and serve it to her in tea. Izzy mentally pushed him higher on the list.

Watson Banks? Roberts defended the doctor who misdiagnosed his late wife. Perhaps it all came back to him when he noticed Roberts on the retreat. They did share a cabin. Yet the forensic team didn't mention finding anything in that kitchenette. But wouldn't Watson have destroyed any evidence?

Sure, that made sense. If Elizabeth or Dr. Barker were guilty, they wouldn't have left stuff lying around the kitchen to incriminate them. Surely not.

General Morton seemed a likely candidate, too, and nothing had been found in his cabin. Not only did he have a temper, but he had also probably killed or ordered the killing of enemies while serving in the Army. After all, wouldn't that make a person numb? Or at least learn to box up the emotions so they could do their duty. Whoever Anthony was, his life seemed to have been ruined by Roberts, which meant a lot to the Mortons. A son or grandson perhaps?

Even so, Izzy had to consider Elizabeth as well. She appeared to be one of the people who leaned toward holistic things. Even in her sixties she'd retained youthful skin and a lean, fit body. But to think she and maybe Miss Fanny planned this thing?

Never. No way could Izzy travel that path no matter how good of friends they were. She shook her head as if that would erase those thoughts entirely.

Shannon came to mind. She often faded into the crowd, but one could never tell about that type of person. Most serial killers were loners, right? And Vernon Roberts had destroyed her husband's business of hand-made longhorn urns.

Oh, good gracious. Any of them could have tried to poison the man. Izzy was getting nowhere. She had to stop all this speculation and read her Bible. *Seriously.*

Chapter Nine

Blend In

Leave it to the sheriff to handle. That's what Izzy's brain told her to do. He struck her as an intelligent man.

Except that he'd left.

But Izzy remained there. And she had the perfect position to eavesdrop. She'd never been considered a tattletale in school and always prided herself in never being known as a gossip, but this didn't seem like prattle. More like information gleaning.

Investigating.

She could use Connie's help, though, especially with the computer searches. But did she fully trust her now? Had Connie eagerly told the police about what Izzy had overheard to divert suspicion from herself?

Though it stung Izzy's heart to think such a thing, she couldn't remove it from the realm of possibility. Truth was, all the people on the retreat, besides her—and hopefully Miss Fanny—were suspects. If she wanted to be of assistance at all she'd have to be an objective observer. This meant keeping an open mind at all costs.

Surely the sheriff's department had people to conduct background checks and the like. Izzy didn't need to get involved in that part of it. No, she could be more useful by keeping a low profile, blending into the wall, and keeping her ears perked.

Miss Fanny pushed herself toward the front door of their cabin. "You are awfully quiet, Izzy. Are you feeling all right?"

"Huh?" Izzy gathered Miss Fanny's shawl in case the dining hall air proved too cool on her frail bones. "Yes. I'm fine. I guess all that has happened today, good and bad, has left my mind rather preoccupied."

Miss Fanny adjusted her purse onto the handle of her rolling walker. "I fully understand. I don't envy Connie trying to reel everyone in tonight. Especially after we have a heavy meal."

And a heavy meal was exactly what the Blakelys had planned. Izzy eyed the marquee in the lobby. It showed a choice of King Ranch Chicken or chicken fried steak with gravy, mashed potatoes, green beans, glazed carrots, jalapeño cornbread, and the choice of a two-inch square chocolate brownie or pecan pie wedge a la mode for dessert. A thick red rope hung in front of the door to the Trough. The staff must have still been preparing the table.

Izzy glanced to the side of the entry hall and noticed Ramona, Janice, and Sally chatting in a conversational grouping off to the left. They all shared an appetizer of nachos. Sally waved at Izzy.

"I think I know one of those gals." Miss Fanny paused as Izzy waved back. "At least she seems familiar."

"If you mean Sally O'Brien, she says you know her mother."

"Aw, yes. Winifred. She and I have served on

a few charity committees together." She diverted her walker. "She and her husband are quite involved in environmental concerns, especially concerning the wetlands. He's a trial attorney if I am not mistaken. I think his daughter is a paralegal with the firm."

Izzy watched her wheel over to say hello then chat for a few minutes.

Connie came from the Paddock Room and joined Izzy. "Looks as if my aunt has new friends."

"Sí. That is Sally O'Brien. Your aunt knows her mother through her charity work. And the one who looks like a model is Ramona Redding."

"Ah, the ex-cheerleader for the Dallas cowboys. I recall the scandal." Connie scrunched her lips to the side.

"Scandal?"

"Seems she hooked up with a wealthy guy at a Dallas pool party and they became an item. His parents hired a private investigator to scoop up any dirt on her." Connie leaned in closer and lowered her voice. "He discovered Ramona lied about her age and altered her driver's license in order to try out for the cheerleaders. The Cowboys fired her, of course, and as a result she also lost a lucrative contract as a diet soft drink spokesperson."

"Wow."

"That's not all. In retaliation, she tried to sue the Zuniga son for rape since she was only fifteen at the time they dated."

Fifteen? How had she put all of that together at such an age? Izzy gave Connie a sidelong look. "How did you learn about all of this?"

Connie scrunched her brow. "Well, beside all the tabloid and news headlines at the time, one member of my prayer group at church knew Alberto Zuniga. They'd been counselors at church camp here in Texas together. He stated that Ramona lied about the extent of their involvement if you get my drift. Alberto remained on our prayer team's list during the month-long trial. We prayed for her as well."

"That was kind of you. Did she lose?"

"Yes." Then suddenly Connie gasped. "Come with me, Izzy." She dashed down the hall. Izzy struggled to keep up with her long, quick strides. They entered the Stallion Room where Connie had her laptop hooked up to the audio-video equipment for the evening's presentation. She crouched on her heels and began clicking her fingernails over the keys.

Izzy hovered close by.

Connie's eyes narrowed, then widened again. "Ah, ha. Guess who Ramona had hired as her attorney?"

"No?" Izzy circled to view the screen.

A newspaper article appeared on the screen, along with a picture of a younger Vernon Roberts. The date on the headlines read 2008. Connie tapped a paragraph at the end. "And look what law firm he was with at the time."

"*O'Brien*, Walters, and Roberts." Izzy's hand pressed against her chest. "Sally's dad? She's a paralegal there. She told me so."

Connie's head tilted toward Izzy's face. "When did you meet them?"

"At the pool this afternoon. They must have arrived just after we did yesterday because I saw them at breakfast this morning."

Connie nodded. "Interesting. Let's see when Vernon left the firm." Within a few minutes she found the answer in an article published in the

Chronicle shortly after the trial. "Here's a quote from Mr. O'Brien. 'We regret that we must disassociate from Vernon Roberts, Attorney at Law. His grandstanding and mudslinging at the Redding versus Zuniga trial hardly fits our image. We want our clients and potential clients to know his behavior is not typical of our firm.'" She pointed at the screen. "How about that? So, two more people staying at the Circle C had a motive. Sally and Ramona."

Connie arched one of her perfectly shaped eyebrows. Then she called Sheriff Tate on her cell phone.

Izzy could hear the call even above the chatter in the Paddock, the laughter echoing in the entry hall, and dishes clinking in the Trough across the way. The sheriff's voice came through surprisingly clear.

"Yes, Miss Wright. Where are you?"

"At the Circle C, of course. In the Stallion Room setting up for tonight's presentation. Why?"

"Because I'm pulling up now. Meet me outside if you would."

She agreed. Izzy saw people had begun to filter into the Trough for dinner. She found Miss Fanny, who already had a full plate before her. "I'll be on the porch with your niece for a few minutes. Will you be all right?"

Miss Fanny nodded with a smile then turned toward Elizabeth who sat on her left.

Izzy made her way through the abandoned hallway. Why was the man back? Could this mean none of the party had guilty hands, including Connie? Someone else had made the attempt? How many enemies had that man made over his career, anyway?

The officer waved and motioned them to have a seat in one of the rows of rockers. He remained standing, however. "Mr. Roberts is better. In fact, they are ready to discharge him."

"Oh?" Connie's eyes enlarged. "Does he have any idea who did this to him?"

"Actually, he has several, as you can well imagine. But no, he doesn't recall anyone approaching his tea while he swam."

"Oh." Her expression deflated.

Izzy's hopes sank as well. Was that what he'd come out to the ranch to tell them? Surely there was more of a reason than that, and he'd been already on the way when Connie called him.

The sheriff cleared his throat. "So, here's the dilemma. He still needs bedrest."

"I gather you don't want him to return here." Connie stated it as a point of fact rather than a question.

"I don't think it would be prudent." The sheriff tilted his cowboy hat back as he leaned against one of the posts. "We have several persons of interest but are not ready to make any arrests. He knows this. He will be staying in a B&B in Mountain Home for two more days then returning to Houston on his own. He's making arrangements for that."

"Okay?" Connie crossed one leg over the other. "And when can the rest of us leave?"

Sheriff Tate's mouth curved on one side as he chewed on a toothpick, again. Maybe gnawing on the thing acted as a stress relief. "You are an intelligent woman. You know this investigation can take a few more days. I've already confirmed with the Blakely's that you can all stay in your rooms through Tuesday afternoon. By then we hope to narrow down our inquiries to one, maybe two persons."

"Then you need to know what we've discovered, which is why I called you in the first place." Connie leaned back with her chin raised.

The sheriff pulled up one of the side tables and sat on it, taking out his notepad. "Very well. Whatcha got?"

She told him about Sally and Ramona's past dealings with the man. "We haven't looked into the other girl's background yet."

"Janice Lewis," Izzy added.

The sheriff wrote in his book.

Connie continued, "It seems they've been close friends for a while. They told Izzy they were sorority sisters."

He closed the notepad and tapped it with the end of his pen. "Well, thank you. I'll definitely speak to them."

Connie gave him a tight smile.

"However, that doesn't alter the current plans." He reached into his pocket. "In fact, I have warrants here to search your group's personal belongings."

Connie grunted, loud enough for Izzy to hear.

Izzy narrowed her eyes. That's why he'd already been on his way here.

"So, if you follow me, we'll inform them that those searches will happen beginning now and continue after dinner while they are together at the presentation you plan to give."

He winked and pulled out a brochure showing the itinerary for the weekend. "That way we will be as little disturbance to your fundraiser as possible."

Connie's mouth curved into a tight smile. "Thank you."

As if they'd received a coded command, two more vehicles' wheels popped over the gravel road heading toward the main building. Six men exited them and walked in the direction of the cabins. Mr. Blakely stepped from the far side of the veranda and joined the group. Sheriff Tate motioned with his head. "We already cleared it with the owners and their attorney."

He must have been out here waiting before Izzy and Connie had exited the building.

The sheriff pulled his phone from a holder on his belt. "Are there any other guests here other than the three ladies and your group?"

Connie shrugged. "Haven't seen any but I wouldn't be the one to ask."

He spoke into the phone. "Melba, with regards to that warrant, amend that to all buildings on the premises."

Izzy and Connie exchanged glances in silence. Did he suspect their hosts? Connie gave Izzy a slight shrug. Izzy returned it.

Connie gracefully unwound her legs. "I suppose we should go tell everyone the news. I imagine they are all still eating dinner. Tonight, they are serving King Ranch Chicken." She rose as the sheriff extended his hand. Then he did the same for Izzy.

Izzy's stomach told her it wouldn't even accept soup at that point. From the expression on Connie's face and the set of her jaw, Izzy doubted she had much of an appetite, either.

Soon, no one would.

Chapter Ten

Dinner Surprise

"Ladies?" The sheriff opened the main door and motioned for them to return to the Trough. Connie and Izzy went to sit with Miss Fanny who gave them a perplexed expression. Before either could respond, a clinking of a spoon on a glass sounded. An officer set the glass down and motioned to the sheriff.

Standing in the entrance to the noisy room, Sheriff Tate looped his thumbs through his belt and spoke in a booming voice. "Ladies and gentlemen." The murmurs of conversations ceased one by one as all eyes fixed on the law enforcement officer. "Mr. Roberts is being released from the hospital this evening. However, he will not be returning to this ranch."

Perplexed faces gazed around the room then back to him. General Morton had the audacity to start clapping in slow beats. Soon Watson and Travis joined in.

Connie bit her lower lip and took in three deep breaths. She appeared ruffled for the first time this weekend. Not that Izzy could blame her, though.

The sheriff whistled through his teeth to end the commotion. "This does not end our investigation." He removed his toothpick and used it as a pointer. "Somebody here at this ranch poisoned the man. Therefore, we are obtaining warrants to search every building on the premises, beginning with each cabin, and this time the search will include your personal belongings."

Murmurs floated through the room.

He lifted his hand and swept the room. "As before, you need to stay in this building until you are dismissed. You are not allowed in your cabins until then." He focused on the three ladies who weren't a part of the retreat. "That includes y'all as well, ladies."

"Us?" Ramona stood. "Why?"

He aimed his glare directly at her. "I think you know why, Ms. Redding. You as well, Ms. O' Brien." He placed the toothpick back in his mouth.

Ramona shut her mouth and slowly sank back into her chair. Sally glanced at her fingernails and Janice's eyes flashed with viciousness.

That's when Izzy finally placed her. Janice Lewis had run for city council and lost due to information leaked by her opponent. Robert Vernon's client, Ted Armstead of the Green Valley Country Club, sued Black Gold Refinery for polluting the ponds and streams on the golf course. The Lewis dynasty had become major shareholders of Black Gold. They eventually won the suit but the damage to her political ambitions had already been done.

Izzy opened her mouth to speak, but the sheriff continued, "And you, Mrs. Lewis. You lost your chance at a seat on the Houston City Council because you were tangled in a lawsuit. In fact, all three of you ladies had run-ins with the notorious Mr. Roberts, correct?"

The others swiveled in their chairs to focus on

the three women sitting in the far corner of the room.

Of course, General Morton blustered first. "Now, see here." He jolted from his chair and took three steps toward the sheriff. "This has gone too far."

The sheriff raised his hand. "Please return to your seat, General." As he'd done before, he matched the man's gaze with an unwavering insistence.

The general heaved a loud exhale and returned to stand beside his table. "I demand to speak to the judge who issued those warrants."

Did he have the right to insist on that? Izzy wasn't sure, but his demand sure made him look more suspicious.

"The Kerr County judge will be in his office at nine o'clock on Monday morning. You can reach him then, but I expect by that time you won't feel the need to call him."

The red-faced man sputtered then returned to his seat.

Yes, the sheriff knew how to handle people.

"Anyone else have a concern?" He eyed each

of them with what seemed to be honest interest.

Travis Thompson raised his hand. "Will we be detained after tomorrow? We were to leave soon after lunch. I'm certain others besides me have meetings or such already planned on Monday."

"Can't answer that, but as soon as I can, I will let you each know so you can make arrangements." He scanned the room as he switched the toothpick to the other side of his mouth. "You might want to call your offices and give them a heads up that you might not be there on Monday, though. Depends on what the searches reveal." He gave a half-smile and pointed toward Travis. "Trust me, my wife would love for me to make an arrest tonight, too. I don't want to be here any longer than y'all do."

He placed his Stetson on his head, a sign Izzy took to mean the conversation had ended. Then he spoke again. "Please enjoy the rest of your dinner and the presentation Miss Wright has prepared for tonight here in the main building. No one leaves the public areas of this complex until I release you to return to your cabins." With a nod of his head, he exited the room.

Connie bent to Miss Fanny's ear. "I don't have

much of an appetite now. I need to make some calls and then speak to the Blakelys."

"Of course, dear."

Izzy watched Connie exit, her cell phone in her hand. What couldn't wait? Did she call her own attorney or change her flight schedule? And why speak to their hosts?

The questions stayed in the back of her head, though she knew she needed to let it go. She started to take a bite of her dinner. Then she halted. Perhaps she shouldn't let it go. She excused herself as well and edged to the doorway then trained her ear to pick up the soft-spoken phone call. Luckily, the lobby was not carpeted and had good acoustics.

"Yes, exactly. This sheriff is no country bumpkin, and he is breathing down my neck." Her tone sounded stern. "I can't gain access right now. I need you to pull this off the rest of the way, okay?"

Connie pocketed her phone and went to find the Blakelys, or so Izzy gathered, with a determined expression plastered on her face and her red pumps echoing her purposeful steps.

What had that been about? Who did Connie

speak with and why would the sheriff put pressure on her? Did he suspect her? Or simply see her as the person in charge?

All of Izzy's squelched suspicions resurfaced and squeezed her stomach into a tight ball that stole her appetite, even though the aromas whiffing from the Trough smelled delicious. Should she tell Sheriff Tate of her unsubstantiated thoughts about Connie? Or would that lead him down a bunny trail away from the real culprit and waste precious time? Maybe earn her a reprimand for sticking her nose where it didn't belong.

Perhaps it would be best all-around if she kept her mouth shut. After all, she really liked her job, and Miss Fanny in particular. And she admired Connie, too. Why jeopardize all of that?

No, if Connie Wright had somehow gotten her thumb stuck in this pie, Izzy didn't want to be the one to pull it out and show everybody.

Lord, show me what to do.

Chapter Eleven

What's in the Food?

"Are you not eating, Izzy?"

Izzy almost jumped out of her shoes when her employer's voice stirred her out of her deep thoughts. "Ay. I didn't hear you, Mees Fanny."

The woman's eyes sparkled. "Well, it isn't like I could sneak up on you." She pushed her wheels forward and then back again to the soft squeaking over the boards. "Where is Connie?"

"Um, she went to speak with the Blakelys about something."

Miss Fanny waved her arm toward the Trough. "Come, get your food. I'm sure she will join us in a minute or so." The expression on Miss Fanny's face demanded obedience, though more of a motherly nature than an employer.

"Yes, ma'am. It's all this upheaval. I'm afraid it's ruined my appetite."

"I understand. But we need to put up a good front for our guests. If we seem off our feed, then it will cause them to worry. That may greatly influence their willingness to support this cause." Miss Fanny laced her arm through Izzy's as she used her other one to push the walker. "No, we must act as if this is no big deal at all. Besides, I know you love King Ranch Chicken. Theirs tastes almost as good as yours."

Izzy knew Miss Fanny made sense. It wouldn't be fair to the sweet children who needed this special care. Especially if everyone in their group turned out to be innocent. Including Connie. Yes, she would put on a brave front and ask the Holy Spirit to guard her thoughts.

But that didn't mean she wouldn't continue to keep her ears sharply tuned.

"Perhaps we shouldn't eat together, then. Maybe if we mingled with the others and kept the conversations positive and light . . ." Wait, what did she just say? That would mean she'd have to engage instead of just listen to the banter going on around her. She almost wished she could swallow the words again.

"Now you're thinking. Great idea." Miss Fanny patted Izzy's hand and wheeled herself back to the table where she'd been sitting with Elizabeth and the Barkers.

This meant Izzy had to choose between the Thompsons and the Mortons, or Watson and Shannon, who suddenly seemed to be in deep conversation.

She reflected on the decision as she filled a salad plate and then a dinner plate. She didn't even pay attention to how much she spooned onto them. Nothing appeared to whet her appetite. With a deep sigh, she turned to face her choice again. The first option would ruin any desire to eat, and the other seemed intrusive.

Three was a crowd, after all.

She tucked her lower lip in her teeth as her eyes darted between the two empty chairs. Eenie, meenie . . .

Shannon's gaze shifted to Izzy. "Oh, do you

need a place to sit? Join us, then."

That was a Godsend. "Are you sure I'm not interrupting?"

Watson stood and pulled out a chair. Then he took one of her plates from her to set on the table. "Not at all. Shannon has been delighting me with her childhood tales of mischief. A teacher she despised for favoritism drank coffee all day long and actually had a pot percolating in the classroom. So, Shannon slipped a liquid laxative in it one day." He snickered and wiped his mouth. "Not exactly dinner conversation but entertaining nonetheless."

When Izzy chuckled, the couple's giggles increased. After a few other stories, the twists in her stomach began to ease.

"Well, I know a man from my church who used to live in China." She had their full attention, and she didn't even feel sick about it. "The man had become increasingly cruel to his manservant. After he moved back here to the US, the man eventually became a Christian and apologized to the servant for the years of abuse. The Chinese servant bowed and said, 'Okay, then. No more spit in soup.'"

Watson laughed so heartedly it made the others in the Trough turn and smile, including a few of the staff.

Izzy grinned. She'd actually told that story pretty well. She glanced at the others who were smiling at her. Then she glanced down. But maybe that meant she wasn't as invisible to people as she thought.

"It feels good to laugh." Shannon gave a final giggle. "Especially considering what's going on in our cabins right now."

Izzy found her voice again. This was the very topic they needed to avoid. "At least none of us are in danger."

"You don't think so?" Watson glanced at Shannon.

Izzy leaned in and took another breath. She could do this. "I think whoever put oleander in Mr. Robert's tea didn't misjudge."

"What do you mean?" Watson set his fork down.

"I think whoever poisoned Vernon Roberts knew exactly how much to give him to make him sick enough to leave the group but not enough to do any real harm."

Shannon didn't reply but glanced at the wallpaper as she sipped some iced tea. The conversation halted for a few seconds. When Shannon noticed Izzy's eyes on her, she set the glass down.

Izzy broke her focus but wondered about the woman's reaction.

Watson chuckled softly, more like a hiccup swallowed in a harumph. "Well, I thank whoever did it. Not having to share a cabin with the guy is quite a pleasant turn of events." He raised his water goblet in a toast. "In fact, in thanksgiving, I plan to donate more than I originally considered."

A melodious voice sounded behind them. "Good news. Thank you, Mr. Banks."

Everyone turned to see Connie smiling down at them. "May I join you?"

Watson's eyes immediately lit up with joy. And Shannon's darkened, or so Izzy thought. Hmm. Not sure how it all fit into this case, or even if it did, but it appeared to Izzy that Shannon had cast her line into Watson's waters hoping for a nibble. And Connie continued to distract him from her bait.

In fact, for the rest of the meal, Connie dominated the conversation while Shannon picked at her green beans and casserole. A gunshot could have gone off and Watson probably wouldn't have lifted his attention from this elegant, poised businesswoman. He almost whipped out his American Express Gold right then and there. Seriously, at one point he reached inside his jacket for his wallet.

Izzy tried to keep from rolling her eyes, then noticed Shannon's focus had shifted to her. A slight smirk grew on the woman's lips, and a devious glint flashed in her eyes. She suddenly shifted in her seat and knocked her iced tea glass over. The contents rushed across the tablecloth toward Connie's lap, too much volume too quickly dumped to be absorbed by the cotton draping.

Connie squealed and jolted from her chair when the liquid hit her lap. She swatted at the stain with her napkin.

Watson padded the table with his own napkin to prevent any further spillage.

Mrs. Blakley appeared out of nowhere. "Here, Connie. Let's go to the ladies' room and do some damage control."

Staff began removing their plates and motioned for Watson, Izzy, and Shannon to move to a vacant table.

Izzy caught Shannon's silent plea not to join them again. "You two finish your meal. I think I'll see if I can help Connie out."

A smooth smile melted Shannon's concern. "Watson, let's have our dessert and coffee by the window so we can watch the sunset."

Izzy shook her head. Poor man seemed doomed. But, by sitting at their table, Izzy had seen a whole new side of the wallflower Shannon. The woman had a calculating mind. Not a shy person at all. More like a cat acting nonchalantly innocent to lure a mouse out into the open.

Could Shannon have been so devious as to remove Vernon Roberts from the scene so Watson could relax and be more susceptible to her charms? After all, she had done something similar to a teacher once.

History may have been repeated. And the

object of her affections might be very grateful to her if it had. He'd even said as much.

Izzy couldn't dash to the police each time a new semi-lead landed in her direction. The sheriff would not appreciate her innuendos and suppositions. No, she needed more proof than a few batted eyelashes and a schoolgirl's story. Or a half-heard, one-sided conversation by the ultra-planner of the bunch, who happened to be her employer's niece.

She tapped on the restroom door. "Do you want me to plead with Sheriff Tate to let you change clothes?"

Connie appeared, completely back in control, besides the round wet spot where the spilled tea had landed on her lap. "No, that's okay, Izzy. Thank goodness I wore durable denim. I plan to dry it with the hands' dryer here in the restroom. Besides, everyone saw it happen, so . . ." She shrugged and closed the door again.

Mrs. Blakley appeared with several dish towels. "We're fine. Go back and enjoy your dessert."

Connie opened the door a wedge and stuck her

head through. "Izzy, be a dear and gather everyone in the Stallion Room in twenty minutes. I realized I still had my evening presentation on a flash drive in my suitcase and, well, we can't have access. Thank the Lord my techie assistant in Chicago has sent the Blakely's the link from my office computer so I can download it onto one of their flash drives instead." She gave the hostess a silent thank-you smile.

Mrs. Blakely blushed. "Where there's a will . . . you know."

So that had been the subject of her hushed phone conversation. And why Connie so eagerly sought out the Blakelys. Izzy almost saluted. And not in a snarky fashion either but in pure admiration. Connie obviously had a take-charge, cool-under-pressure personality.

"Nothing fazes you, Connie, does it?"

She answered with a wink. "Not for long. God is in control, and I believe these charities are doing His will. I'm only a small instrument in His plan. I learned a long time ago that getting flustered over the little detours only blocks the Holy Spirit's flow."

Izzy felt a warm tingle glide through her heart. A woman who relied on the Almighty wouldn't take matters into her own hands, especially devious ones that could cause harm. Izzy almost apologized to her for her swirling thought accusations. However, Connie spoke up first.

"Now, go get everyone gathered and tell them that our evening activities will begin soon. I'll be there in two shakes of a lamb's tail. That's what my mother used to say."

Connie gave Izzy a thumbs up, took the towels from Mrs. Blakely, and disappeared deeper into the ladies' room.

Mrs. Blakley waved her arm. "You heard the lady. Head 'em up, move 'em out."

Wait. What? She couldn't go into that room full of people and make an announcement. Even if she tried, no one besides herself would hear her.

Izzy walked into the Trough. She stood inside the door as both Connie and the sheriff had done. "Uh, excuse me."

That didn't even make a dent in the conversations and the general hum around the room.

"Uh, ladies and gentlemen."

No better. She moved to the buffet line and picked up a couple of plates. She clapped them together making a whacking noise until the hum began to die down. Then she looked around at all the faces staring at her. She could do this.

She took a deep breath. "The . . . the presentation will . . ."

"We can't hear you." Travis Thompson stood at the back of the room.

"The presentation," she called to him as though he was the only one she spoke to. "It will begin shortly in the Stallion Room. Please make your way there, now."

She stopped. Low and behold, the patrons began to stand and collect jackets, shawls, and purses. She'd done it. A grin surged up from her toenails and spread across her face.

Others were grinning as well.

Izzy couldn't help but sense the momentum shift to the positive. Perhaps like she, the others in the room recalled the good things that happened that day. The smiles and giggles of the children as they rode around the ring echoed in her mind. As did Connie leaping over the jumps in the corral and Miss Fanny's glee when the Sandersons helped her onto the back of a horse. Despite all the rigmarole of the investigation into Vernon Robert's poisoning, the retreat had been a success so far.

The Visitor Makes a Retreat

Chapter Twelve

Found It.

Perhaps because they had nothing else to do while the police searched their cabin, the three young women joined the group for Connie's wrap-up presentation.

Izzy watched them. At first, they whispered together, seemingly with no interest in the presentation, but as the lights dimmed and Connie's video came up, their expressions changed. All three of them were as engaged as the patrons when stories of two of the children were displayed on the screen.

At the end of the presentation, the room exploded in applause as the lights returned to their original brightness. Izzy noticed Miss Fanny's eyes had reddened at the rims, as did several of the patron's including General Morton of all people.

Connie quietly handed a brochure with a pledge form and envelope to each person in the room, including the younger trio.

Then after a few murmurs the room fell silent. The sound of pens scratching across paper as heads dipped to the tables made Connie's face glow, and not from the projector's light.

Well done. Izzy caught Connie's eye and gave her a nod.

The smile Connie returned beamed with sincere warmth and love for this charity. It made Izzy so uncomfortable about her previous suppositions she proceeded to write a small check to the charity herself, almost as an act of penance. She then slipped it into the basket at the back of the room and went to stand on the long veranda for some fresh, spring evening air.

One by one, most of the patrons followed suit, some finding a rocker to sit in while others gathered in small groups to chat. Izzy wrapped her arms around her waist and watched their facial expressions. The tension of the morning had disappeared.

And Izzy had to admit Watson had been correct. The removal of the thorn in their flesh had saved the retreat. In hindsight, it hardly seemed a crime.

Then a shout shattered the pleasant atmosphere. Flashlights darted over the ranch like disorientated fireflies. Men in uniform rushed to the sound of the shout. But they headed away from the patrons' cabins toward the other side of the pool area. The glow of the aqua ripples shimmering above underwater lights softly illuminated their shadowy figures.

Sally gasped and Janice pointed into the darkness, dotted by patches of illumination from strategically placed spotlights throughout the ranch. "They're headed to our cabin." In unison, they dashed toward their quarters ignoring the sheriff's words.

Almost as if directed by a movie producer, the rest of the people shuffled after them, despite the previous admonishment to stay in the main building.

When Miss Fanny moved down the accessibility ramp, Izzy could only follow her.

The women had been stopped and sent back to the main house, but they lingered at the end of the pool near the large jacuzzi. The patrons joined them there and Izzy helped Miss Fanny to the group as well.

The rhythmic lapping of the water seemed to only heighten Izzy's senses. As she watched in silence, the faces near her reflected her own anxiety.

"What are they doing in our cabin?" Sally held her head in her hands.

"How dare they rummage through our personal things." Janice stomped her foot.

"If you don't stop, I'm calling my attorney." Ramona called out and waved her phone at one of the officers.

The sheriff came out of the well-lit cabin and strode to the pool. "Who owns the pink-flowered luggage?"

"I do." Ramona raised her hand, and her chin.

Izzy eased closer to the trio.

"Want to explain why several sprigs of

oleander were wrapped in cellophane and placed in the inside pocket?" The sheriff pulled out his notepad and a pen. "And why your laptop had an article on oleanders displayed on its screen?"

Ramona's arms formed a pretzel over her chest, and she rebelliously flounced into a deck chair beside the pool. "It so happens that oleander sap has medicinal benefits. The elixir has been known to relieve flu symptoms such as headaches, muscle aches, and congestion. Which, if you had taken the time to read my screen, you would now know, sheriff." She narrowed her eyes at his face when she spoke his title.

The man's body language didn't change. "And?"

She wiggled in her chair. "I'm thinking of expanding my product line and wanted to take a few samples back to my lab boys. See if we could develop it into a cream for migraines and minor pain relief."

"I see."

"With all these viruses running rampant over the world, my product could provide homeopathic relief. No costly prescriptions needed. No trips to the doctor. Safe for children. It could be a gold mine." She cocked her head. "And be a huge benefit to humanity, of course."

"Of course." The sheriff's voice didn't indicate he'd been convinced by her spiel. "And so, you figured that was reason enough to pluck them from the grounds without permission?"

"That's exactly what I did. But I had permission."

Sally spoke up. "We were all together on this project's possibilities. We asked the gardener, José, if we could take some after he'd trimmed the hedges."

The sheriff whistled to his deputy. "Go find this gardener, José. Bring him here."

José? The man she'd seen the other evening didn't have a hint of anything Hispanic in him. His hair had been a little on the mousy side, but he seemed very light-skinned. He wasn't even tanned. That was what niggled in the back of her mind about him. An inconsistency. Most gardeners, working in the sun all day, would show something of a tan on their hands or faces.

The deputy left to carry out the order. The

sheriff shifted his attention back to Ramona.

"And naturally you boiled some of the leaves down to try it on yourself."

"Yes. I let it cool and then mixed it into my rose cream. I do experience headaches." She rubbed her temple in tight circles.

"And you did this when?"

"Friday. Late in the afternoon. We had arrived after lunch. We were tired and a bit sweaty, so we decided to take a dip before dinner."

Janice laid a hand on her friend's arms. "That's when she saw the gardener trimming the oleander back. She called to him and asked the name of the plant. When he told her it was oleander, she got all excited."

"I'd been reading about it just the other day," Ramona said. "It was like the heavens opened up." She flitted her manicured claws in the air and sung out a long-pitched note.

The sheriff dragged a chair over and sat down.

The screech across the concrete made Izzy cringe. She and Miss Fanny had slowly made their way forward during the sheriff's conversation with Ramona.

Connie joined them. "She had oleander in her room?"

Izzy nodded as the sheriff continued. "And in your research did you also discover that it could have harmful effects to the heart and stomach?"

Ramona flipped her dark ponytail behind her shoulder. "Well, yes. But we'd only used a few tiny drops in the cream. My lab boys would figure out the ratio. That's why I pay them the big bucks." She leaned back and crossed one leg over the other. With both arms and legs crossed, she resembled one of those crisscross barricades Izzy had seen in old war movies. "It is only one of the expansions I am considering. You did notice the bag of Fredericksburg peaches, I assume? They are known for their vitamin C and antioxidants. And the wild mustang grapes that grow along the riverbanks here? They contain Resveratrol."

The sheriff, for once, seemed lost for words. The deputy rounded the side of the main building with a man in workman's clothes that had a layer of dirt and dust on them.

When they neared the sheriff, the deputy leaned over to speak to his boss.

The other man slouched and kept his head down, but he stood silently for a moment and then erupted. "I don't know what you want from me."

Mr. Blakley trotted down the steps, aiming directly for the sheriff. "What is this all about? Why has my gardener been collected? He was only eating dinner."

So this was the man who had been digging in the garden. Izzy eyed him, but with his head down and his shoulders all hunched over, she couldn't tell any more about him than when she first saw him in the dark the other night.

The sheriff gave him a sidelong look. "This is about poison, sir. As you well know." He glanced from Mr. Blakely to the trio of girls and back again. "And it looks like your goddaughter, Ramona, is in the thick of it."

What? Izzy's mouth dropped open. As did Connie's.

Chapter Thirteen

Grudges

The events seemed surreal to Izzy, as if she watched a TV crime show unfold. But then, she'd not had that much run-in with crime investigations.

Deputy Amos approached. "We've finished searching your cabins, folks. You can return to them now. On behalf of the Kerr County Sheriff's Office, thank you for your cooperation." With a tip of his Stetson, he stepped away.

"I suppose that means that the magnifying glass is off of us now." General Morton harrumphed. "Come on, Brooke. I've had enough drama for one day."

His wife sputtered but shuffled after his long

strides.

Travis Thompson turned to his wife. "I agree. Looks as if those gals did the dirty work for us." He snickered but his humor fell flat. "Um, Carolyn? You want to stay?"

"For a moment." She scanned the ones who remained. "Why on earth would that young lady poison the man?"

Shannon, who had been hanging on Watson's arm for support, replied to the whole group. "Don't y'all know? She was that Dallas Cowboy cheerleader who was fired for being underage. Ramona's fiancé broke up with her. He's the son of a big-time Dallas real estate agent, Oscar Zuniga. A real catch. She'd lied to him as well, about a lot of things. Plus . . ." she whispered loudly, ". . . they said she had, you know, relations with several of the football players."

"Shannon." Watson gave her a disgusted expression and removed her hand from his arm.

Carolyn sniffed. "What does that have to do with Vernon Roberts?"

Shannon straightened her shoulders and gave a pout in Watson's direction. She proceeded to explain how Roberts had tried to defend Ramona but raked her through the mud instead and ruined her budding career.

Connie stepped forward. "But why blame Mr. Roberts? She herself brought on her own fall from grace lying about her age and probably about the rest of it as well."

Izzy piped up. "People curse the police who stop them from speeding all the time."

"Well, it appears her two friends held grudges as well." Shannon pointed to the girls. "See the one sitting opposite Ramona? Sally O'Brien. I know her mother. You do, too, right Miss Fanny? Her father was head of the law firm that had hired Roberts."

Carolyn gasped. "I remember that. It made all the papers. Roberts made such a grandstanding fool of himself in front of the national press that he tarnished the firm's reputation, and they let him go. That's when he moved to Houston."

Shannon nodded. "And then there is Janice Lewis."

Carolyn cocked her head to the side. "Wasn't she running for city council not too long ago?"

Shannon bobbed her head several times and reiterated how the lawsuit damaged her oil dynasty. And now that she thought about it, hadn't Vernon Roberts represented the other side?

Connie stepped up. "Ladies, this is all speculation. I am sure the sheriff and his men will sort it out. It obviously doesn't concern us or our reason for being here."

Izzy didn't feel as confident about that.

Miss Fanny decided to wheel away from the conversation at this point. Izzy wobbled on her feet, torn between staying to hear more and following her to the cabin. She scurried to her employer's side. "Mees Fanny. I will be in shortly. I must speak with Connie about something first."

The old woman nodded and slowly edged away from the pool area. She appeared more bent over than normal. Likely from the weight of all this.

Watson curled his upper lip. "I have heard enough dirty tales out of school. Good night." He stomped off with his hands thrust deep in his pockets.

Shannon stood with her mouth partially open.

Seemed to Izzy that perhaps she had just fallen from grace as well in the eyes of Watson Banks. Then Izzy noticed Shannon's eyes flicker to the same officer that had dismissed them. Amos. He'd been hanging off to the side but still within earshot range. He slowly turned on his heel and sauntered over to the sheriff. As he did, Shannon's eyes followed him, and her mouth curved into a little satisfied smirk.

Whoa. Shannon was even more calculating than Izzy figured. She touched Connie's elbow. "Can I speak with you about something?"

"Sure."

The two moved away from the others, no longer focused on the diminishing drama at the poolside. In the semi-dark shadows Izzy told Connie about the dinner conversation before she had arrived, and how she'd observed the deputy hanging around the perimeter of the group to hear Shannon's gossip before moving back to the poolside.

"Should I tell Sheriff Tate?" Izzy felt like a child, but she didn't want to be accused of playing the games that Shannon seemed to be playing.

"You think Shannon purposely slandered those ladies to draw attention from herself?"

"She had plenty of motive for poisoning Vernon Roberts. She blamed him for her husband's despondency and early death. Is not the phrase, *Revenge is a dish best served cold*?"

"Well, perhaps, but . . .?" Connie stopped and turned toward the pool. "Wait a minute. Look."

Izzy turned to see Deputy Amos lead a very verbal Ramona away in handcuffs. "Uncle Bob. Stop them. They can't do this. Call our attorney."

As the deputy put her in one of the cruisers, the other police at the scene began to disperse.

Bob Blakely shuffled toward the main building with his head down. The gardener shuffled away, probably glad not to be interviewed any more.

And Shannon walked away with a huge grin on her face.

Connie thrust a hand to her right hip. "Now why did they do that?"

"I think we know." Izzy motioned with her head to the retreating Shannon. "I have one more question."

"Okay?"

Izzy turned to Connie. "It is about the gardener. If he had trimmed the oleanders on the Friday afternoon and given the branches to Ramona, why did he rake the clippings so late that night while we chatted in the Canteen."

"Where?" Connie scanned the area.

Izzy pointed to the far end.

"Bingo." Connie touched the tip of her nose with one hand and pointed at Izzy with the other. "Good observation. Go ahead and get Aunt Fanny tucked in for the night. Then, change into grubbier clothes and meet me over there in an hour. Let's find out."

Izzy rushed to catch up to her employer. "Come on, Mees Fanny. You have had a long day. A warm bath and you will be ready to climb under the covers."

"I have rarely heard more marvelous words. I am so glad you thought to bring that fold-up shower chair and sprayer wand." She patted Izzy's hand. "What would I ever do without you, dear?"

Izzy bent to kiss the old woman's wrinkled cheek. Over the past few years, as sisters in Christ, they had bonded into more than employee and employer. She knew her client's years on earth were on the downward trend, but she sent up a prayer to extend them a bit longer. Eighty seemed a lot younger than it once had. And the woman's wit remained sharp.

She lathered the washcloth with Miss Fanny's favorite lavender soap and left the woman to wash herself in the tub enclosure while she turned the bed down.

"You seem to be pondering deep thoughts," Miss Fanny called from the other room. "I sense that you don't think Ramona Redding is the culprit."

"I am not sure." Izzy helped her from the tub and wrapped her in a large towel. "The evidence stacks up against her, but Connie and I were able to catch most of her explanation, and it sounded reasonable."

She relayed about the deputy overhearing Shannon's mantra and then returning to arrest Ramona. "Two things seemed strange to me about that. The first is that Bob Blakely is her godfather, whom she calls *uncle*. Of course, it could be that is why she and her friends met up here for their reunion."

"Hmm, yes. I imagine they'd get a hefty, discounted rate. And often people call men closely knitted to the family uncle, even though they are not blood relatives."

"True." Izzy shrugged. "And I guess it could be a coincidence that they booked the same weekend in which Vernon Roberts would be here with us. When Ramona saw him arrive, she would have had to plot this whole poison thing, though. If so, she would have to be a very quick thinker."

"Hmm. Seems unlikely but I guess stranger things have happened. But if she had acted, why just poison him enough to get him away from the ranch?"

Izzy smiled as she lifted the nightgown over the woman's head and smoothed it down to her knees. "Exactly. Why not 'do him in'. That is the term, is it not?"

Miss Fanny chuckled. "Well, you heard her tell the sheriff she'd leave the appropriate amounts to her lab boys. Maybe she underestimated what it would take."

"Perhaps. I can see the police thinking so." She helped Miss Fanny into her bed and pulled the covers over her.

"You said two things seemed odd to you, my dear."

Izzy paused, reflecting on what she'd seen the previous night. "The gardener, José, was sweeping up the trimmings around the oleanders after sunset last night. It was odd timing, but it might have only been an oversight."

"It could be he was called away and returned after dinner to finish up. I think he may have helped everyone with their luggage when we arrived, come to think of it."

"Really?" Izzy admitted she hadn't noticed. Like her, other menial workers were often overlooked. She inwardly scoffed. She had been guilty of the same thing that she had often secretly chastised others for doing.

Miss Fanny fluffed her pillow. "As you said, perhaps he didn't want to disturb the guests who use the pool. I gather early afternoon to shortly before dinner would be prime time for swimming. Plus, once the sun is down the temperature is cooler in the evening. He may very well have had his dinner, then returned to complete his chore. The Blakelys run a tight ship from what I've seen."

Miss Fanny always looked to the positive. It could have been just like that. "You are a wise woman. Even so, Connie and I are going to snoop around in a bit."

"Well, then you better get going. My niece doesn't like to be kept waiting." Miss Fanny winked and pulled the covers over her shoulders. "Just be careful."

"Sí. Good night, Mees Fanny." Izzy flicked off the bedside table lamp and closed the door, leaving it open slightly in case her client needed her in the night.

Then she changed into jeans and a Binge Jesus t-shirt, grabbed her flashlight, and slipped through the private patio gate to meet Connie.

What she expected to discover escaped her. Miss Fanny's explanation about the gardener made sense. Especially if he resided on the ranch.

His actions could be totally innocent.

Still, she couldn't shake her suspicion that the sheriff had the wrong suspect sitting in his jail.

Chapter Fourteen

Something's Brewing

As she walked to the canteen, Izzy phoned the front desk and asked if it would be okay to take a late-night swim.

"Of, course. The pool doesn't close until eleven on weekends."

"Oh, good. I asked because I noticed the gardener, what's his name?"

"José?" The receptionist's reply held a question behind it. Not that she didn't know the name but perhaps why Izzy wanted to learn it.

"Yes, José. Anyway, he was raking and trimming the bushes last evening about this time, and I thought perhaps he did that when the pool closed in order to not disturb the guests."

"Oh, I see. Okay." She hesitated for a moment. "Can I help you with anything else?"

Izzy picked up the receptionist's change in tone. She wouldn't get anything else out of the woman.

"No. Thank you, and good night."

Connie stood waiting for her. Izzy waved and walked over to her.

"Shall we do some digging?" She winked.

"Ready. And I phoned the front desk and asked if it would be all right for us to be at the pool because I had seen the gardener last evening and thought perhaps, he worked only after pool hours."

Connie chuckled. "My, aren't we clever. What did they say?"

"It is what she did not say that struck me as odd. As if she had no clue why he would be out here. But of course, she would not reveal that to a guest."

"Interesting." Connie beckoned Izzy to follow her past the Canteen. "Before we snoop around the bushes, let's query Ramona's friends. Tell them we think her to be innocent and see what they say."

Izzy liked that idea. "I will let you do the talking, then." She held her hand across her torso. Her stomach still felt a bit fluttery. After all, she'd spoken more in one evening than she did for a solid week most of the time.

"Well, their cabin still has lights on, so let's give it a shot."

Connie tapped her fingernails on the door, the loud clicks resounding against the concrete porch. Sally answered, her nose slightly red as if she'd been crying.

Connie titled her head in empathy. "We're sorry to barge in like this, but we think the sheriff made a poor assumption about Ramona. Over the past day I've developed a rapport with him as head of this fundraising retreat. I think he might listen to me." She paused and let her words soak in.

The facial wrinkles on Sally's forehead eased, but she didn't let go of the doorknob. "Oh?"

"May we come in and chat?"

She rubbed a hand down her hair. "Um, yeah. I guess. Let me get Janice." She opened the door wider and stepped back.

Connie and Izzy entered and sat on the sofa.

They could hear the two women murmur together in the bedroom farthest from the door. Then they both appeared. Janice sat down and spoke first.

"You want to speak to the sheriff?"

"Well, we think Ramona could be innocent. Izzy and I sat chatting at the pool yesterday evening and the gardener, José, lingered. He trimmed some of the oleander bushes and then raked up the leaves and hauled them off. Did Ramona ask for more last night?"

The two women glanced at each other and shook their heads in unison.

"Hmm." Connie crossed her legs. "Then I wonder why he decided to finish his yardwork so late. Any ideas?"

"No clue." Janice inched forward in the armchair. "I know Ramona asked him for clippings earlier in the day. But he brought those by in the afternoon. When he asked why, she showed him the website. They chatted about it for a while."

Connie tapped her fingernail to her chin.

Izzy's head spun. It almost sounded as though Ramona gave the man the idea. But what on earth would he have against Vernon Roberts?

Sally lifted one slender shoulder. "Ramona didn't poison the man. Seems to me a lot of us hated the guy. Did you two ever have any run-ins with his shyster-like methods?"

"No." Izzy glanced at the rug.

"I'm from Chicago." Connie chimed in. "I only came down here to raise money for the Equine Engage, with Aunt Fanny's help of course." Connie narrowed her eyes. "Neither of you poisoned him, I assume?"

"No!" Sally spoke first. "My father owned the firm Vernon Roberts first joined. He took on Ramona's case because we were in the same sorority in college. Gave it to Roberts like throwing a bone to a dog. Thought it might boost the man's career and as Daddy said, he had fire in his gut." She smoothed the seam of her shorts and didn't glance up again. "Instead, Roberts made a mockery of the system with his grandstanding and slandering the football players' reputations. The press had a field day with him. You know how Dallas loves the Cowboys. Anyway, Daddy fired Roberts because his love for the cameras tarnished the firm's reputation."

Connie's perfectly shaped mouth pouted. "That's why he relocated to Houston. Houston does not necessarily love the Cowboys."

"Definitely." Janice rose. "Want something to drink?" She let off a nervous laugh. "Nothing brewed. Promise. We have orange juice, Diet Cokes, and stevia-sweetened lemonade."

Connie asked for the lemonade and Izzy decided on the same.

She returned with a tray of four tumblers and the pitcher. As she poured, she told them about her dealings with the man. Of course, none of her story was new to Izzy, and she'd already shared what she knew with Connie, but they listened and sipped from their glasses.

When she finished, Connie set her drink on the end table. "Are you bitter?"

"Not anymore. For a long time, yes. But I think of it now as a blessing." She smiled. "Daddy pushed me into politics. I'd always been involved in the student councils in school, even into college. He thought I had great potential and being the youngest city council member of Pearland would be only a steppingstone."

"But your heart never caught up, right?"

"No, it didn't." She took a long drink of the lemonade.

Sally gave her friend a sympathetic smile. "It's tough having socially powerful parents. So much to live up to, so much that people expect. I know well enough." She gave a small chuckle half-hidden in a scoff.

"I understand. I inherited the foundation and grew up with it almost as if it became a family member." Connie uncrossed her legs and leaned forward. "At first it seemed obligatory. Not in a bad way, mind you. More of an assumption. My mother had me late in life. As the youngest child by years, running the foundation naturally fell into my lap when my parents wanted to retire. But somewhere along the process it became my passion. I think God touched my heart while I was in college."

"I wish I could say the same." Janice lifted her eyes from Connie's face and stared out the window into the night.

Sally sighed and pressed her back further into the sofa. "Dad always planned for me to be in his firm. I'm the substitute for the son he never had, I guess. Luckily, women are more accepted in the ol' boys' club nowadays. I don't mind. As his paralegal, I get to do a lot of research."

Izzy felt totally lost in the conversation between these power-women. But she didn't want to get up and leave, either. She decided to sit, enjoy her drink, and listen. Maybe she'd learn something.

Connie took another sip from her glass and shifted in her seat. "Now that the dust has settled, Janice, have you other plans?"

She met Connie's gaze. "Actually, I am glad you stopped by. Your presentation touched me tonight." Janice placed her hand over her heart, and her eyes became watery. "I want to become involved in your foundation. I really am good at public relations, and I'd love to help raise money for your charities."

Izzy could tell that Janice's statement came as a total surprise to Connie. Of course, it could be a ploy to throw them off her scent. The woman seemed sincere, though.

Connie took a long drink before responding. "Of course, you would have to be vetted. Are you seeking a paid position?"

"Not necessarily. I have enough to live on for the moment. I am still involved with Black Gold's P.R. work. Slowly we are bouncing back and showing the communities in the area we are environmentally conscientious. But I could take on something else, too. Perhaps even relocate."

"I see."

Janice sucked in a deep breath. "You don't see. Not entirely, I mean. I can't have children of my own, and I think helping kids in need might be a balm for my pain."

"Oh, I am sorry." Connie wet her lips. For the first time, Izzy thought perhaps she had lost her words. Could something similar be the reason why Connie never married? Or was she simply married to the foundation?

Janice recovered her emotions with a stronger voice and straighter spine. "You're a savvy businesswoman, Connie Wright. But I promise you I do have qualifications. I have been locally involved in fundraising for various children's concerns." She counted them off on her fingers. "CASA, otherwise known as the child advocacy in court program, the Children's Miracle Network, Head Start, and Texas Children's Hospital in Houston. I'll admit, at first my involvement had a selfish motive, to reinvent myself. But like you, somewhere along the way my heart began to beat again."

Connie's face brightened. "Very well. In the morning I will drop off my card and a few brochures and we'll talk soon. Just realize this is a godly-focused foundation. I'll want you to review our statement of faith thoroughly before we proceed."

"Of course."

All four women rose. Sally stopped Connie and Izzy. "So, are you going to talk to the sheriff?"

Izzy turned to Connie. Were they?

Connie answered without a blink. "Yes, of course. In the morning. But first, I want to do a bit more research on José. I mean, what would be his motive?"

Janice and Sally exchanged glances and then shrugged.

Connie stepped through to the porch. "Good night, ladies. I'm glad we talked."

As they walked back to the pool area, Izzy asked for her impressions.

Connie hummed for a second before answering. "Well, I think Janice might be sincere, especially about wanting to be involved with the foundation. I need to do some surfing on her. It could be a red herring."

"A what?"

"Red herring. In the early 1800s criminals used smoked fish to draw bloodhounds away from their scent. Or so the story goes. So, a red herring, which is a powerfully odiferous smoked fish, became known as anything used to distract someone from discovering the truth."

"Oh, I see."

Connie indicated with her head for Izzy to glance in the direction of the shadowy oleanders. Enough light shimmered from the pool to partially illuminate the bases of their trunks. "But first, let's see if José buried something he didn't want to be found."

To Izzy's surprise, Connie hurried over, knelt on the pebbly concrete, and began moving the dirt with her fingers. So much for her expensive-looking manicure and gelled nails. The fact this lady didn't mind getting her hands dirty became a comfort and a concern at the same time. Why did she seem so earnest in shining the light on this gardener?

Maybe being surrounded by power and influence this weekend had made her skeptical that anyone could be aboveboard and honest. Except Miss Fanny. Despite her social status, the woman radiated sincerity. Then again, Connie B. Wright constantly surrounded herself with these types of people. Why the fervor, then? Curiosity, or something more personal? Izzy suddenly realized she didn't know if Connie had any connections to Vernon Roberts.

Why would she? It was probably Izzy's own insecurity being with such a wealthy crowd that clouded her judgment. Perhaps it was time for her to step back into the shadows for a moment.

Izzy went over to help. "What are we looking for?"

"No idea. Something that doesn't belong in the soil underneath oleanders, I guess." Connie kept sifting through the mulch and dirt. A slight whiff of manure floated up, and it made Izzy choke.

"Not used to horse poop, eh?" Connie eyed her and then returned her attention to the soil. "For me the odor brings back fond memories at my aunt and uncle's ranch. Mucked many a stall during those visits."

Her lemonade made a reappearance in Izzy's throat as she started to dig. Then her fingers hit something hard.

"Connie? I think I found something."

The two dug in the same spot. Connie let out an ah-hah and held up a dark brown glass bottle by the eye dropper's rubber bulb screwed into the top. "I'm guessing this isn't for swimmer's ear."

She handed it to Izzy, telling her not to touch the glass but to hold it only with her fingernails by the stopper top. Then she dug her phone from her hip pocket and called Sheriff Tate.

Chapter Fifteen

Along for the Ride

Connie put the call on speaker so Izzy could hear the conversation.

"Exactly why were you digging in the bushes at this hour of the night?" Sheriff Tate didn't sound pleased.

"Because we thought it odd for a gardener to be working so late in the evening."

Izzy added her part, "And the receptionist didn't confirm it to be normal behavior."

"So, we figured he might be up to something." Connie met Izzy's gaze and nodded. "Afterall, he gave the oleander leaves to Ramona."

"That hardly makes him an accomplice."

"True, but—"

"You should have notified me instead of proceeding, Miss Wright. We have forensic teams skilled at this sort of thing." His tone dripped with frustration. "You may have done more damage than good. I will send one of my team over. I need you to stop what you're doing and wait for us."

The click startled Izzy, but Connie simply saluted the phone. She obviously didn't cotton to being tongue-lashed.

Izzy broke out laughing. So much of the day's tension melted from her shoulders. She covered her mouth, realizing the sounds echoed off water. "Sorry . . . I guess we sit here until the officer arrives?"

Connie arched one eyebrow. "Guess so. Let's go sit in the Canteen." She sashayed away toward the shadowed, open area filled with tables and chairs. Clearly, the sheriff's attitude had irritated her.

Izzy followed and set the little bottle on the table near the small floral centerpiece. "At least this time, none of your guests need to know about another deputy's visit."

"True. I can hardly believe there was so much support for the charity after having this place become an angry ant bed of law enforcement officials."

"Well," Izzy patted her hand. "You did all you could do to try to shield the patrons from what was happening."

They had only been at the table for a few moments when a shadowed figure approached. It was a tad too curvy to be a forensic retriever. And in a robe.

Elizabeth stepped into the dim light and pulled her fleece lounger tighter around her waist. "There you are, Connie. You weren't in the cabin. Then I heard voices. May I join you two?"

Connie glanced at Izzy, her eyes speaking volumes.

Izzy shrugged. A deputy would be there any moment. "Sure, pull up a chair." Connie glanced back at the woman.

They couldn't very well explain what they were doing there though. "So many wonderful things happened today. Despite all the disruptions."

"Oh yes, I actually enjoyed the afternoon."

Elizabeth's smile widened. "And your presentation tonight stirred me, Connie. Truly. Well done."

Izzy agreed. "The children's reaction delighted my heart today, too. In person and in the video."

"Thank you, ladies. I so love my job." Connie tipped her head. "But when the Sandersons helped Aunt Fanny onto a horse, it made my year. Captured it in a video with my phone and plan to send it to all my siblings." Connie scrolled her finger over the screen. "Here. See?"

Elizabeth bent to peer at the images and smiled even more. "What a sweet grin on her face. Like a kid given the keys to the ice cream truck."

Izzy viewed it as well. That's when she noticed something strange. Zac Sanderson didn't smile. In fact, his face appeared blank, as if his mind had been preoccupied. Perhaps he had a case of jitters over trying to influence such prominent and potentially profitable people. It could be that his wife, Judy, handled the public relations end. She did seem to be very personable and outgoing.

As a couple in business together, it would make sense. He handled the horses, she, the people. Judy pitched the program while he came along for the ride, as it were.

Still the reflection in Zac Sanderson's eyes showed another emotion Izzy couldn't quite grasp. Not exactly anger, not quite wariness. She wondered if the police crawling around put him on edge for some reason. Did he have a past?

If he did, surely Connie would know. Izzy couldn't imagine her not vetting the charities in her foundation very, very closely.

And it would be difficult to ask her about that. *Oh, by the way, why does one of your charity heads seem nervous around cops?* It would almost be as if she evasively asked if Connie's foundation laundered money, smuggled drugs, or had mob connections. How would she take it?

No, this Izzy would have to investigate on her own. But how? The Sandersons had already left hours ago. She could call and say one of the patrons had a question. Nope. Again, it might come across as accusatory. So much for the old-fashioned way.

Time to learn more about surfing the web.

Connie leaned across the table with her hands folded. "You're awfully quiet, Izzy."

Izzy jerked, realizing Connie and Elizabeth's chatter, previously faded to background noise, had stopped entirely.

It wouldn't do to explain what she had been thinking. She stretched out both arms to the side and then covered her mouth with a mock yawn. "I admit that I am beginning to feel the effects of such a filled day and so much drama."

"Funny, I'm not sleepy a bit. Maybe because of the drama. I just can't see that poor little girl poisoning the man." Elizabeth scrunched her nose. "Even if he was a creep."

Izzy turned at the sound of footsteps. The sheriff or his deputy? How would they explain that? She reached for Elizabeth's hands to pull her to standing. "Perhaps you should try a glass of milk? There is some in one of the snack bars in the main building."

"That's a wonderful idea." Connie stood as well.

"Thanks, but no." Elizabeth waved their hands away. "I am lactose intolerant, girls. Even before it was in fashion." She chuckled and turned to leave.

A man approached and flashed a badge. "Good

evening, ladies." He nodded at each of the women and gave a tug on the cowboy hat that had been pulled down over low on his forehead.

Elizabeth whirled around.

"Good evening." Connie picked up the centerpiece, revealing the little bottle that they'd hidden there.

The deputy remained where he was, but he seemed to be writing something on a notepad. "That's it, huh?"

Connie nodded and folded her arms over her waist. They watched as he put on gloves and then opened a sack with a red zip-lock seal. He reached over and picked up the vial with a pair of tweezers then slipped it inside the baggie.

Pressing it shut, he stepped back. "Anything else?"

Connie sat forward. "No. I mean we stopped digging when we discovered that. It just now occurred to me that there may be more evidence over there." Connie twisted her torso and pointed to the third bush on the left.

As if in response to her voice, a swift breeze slithered through the pool area and rustled the slender green leaves of the oleander bushes. Soothing yet a tad eerie at the same time. The pool ripples waved over the submerged lights. The slight scent of chlorine mixed with fruity sweetness of the orange-pink oleander blossoms flitted in the air, colliding with Elizabeth's powdery lavender perfume and a hint of a musky aftershave. Probably the deputy's.

"We may get some weather tonight. Thunderstorms to the west." His voice sounded a little familiar. Probably one of the deputies who had been there during the day. "Got a bit of time before it hits, I guess. Well, doesn't hurt to look." He extracted a flashlight from his utility belt and headed to the edge of the concrete. Connie followed him toward the spot.

Elizabeth grabbed Izzy's arm. "What is all this about?"

Izzy shook her head. "I do not know anything for certain. We found something in the bushes over there." She shrugged and then followed the bobbing light to the other side of the pool. She didn't have to look to see if Elizabeth followed her. The shuffling sound of her house shoes on the deck confirmed it. Even so, in the stillness of the night the deputy's and Connie's voices carried across the ripples.

Crouching down to balance on his cowboy boots, the deputy began to move the beam of light across the mulch. The glow rested on a mound of disturbed dirt. "It had been buried?"

Connie waved her finger over the open space. "Yes, about two to three inches under the mulch."

He mumbled an "uh-huh" then rose back to his full height, keeping the light focused on the spot. "And how did you know where to look?"

Connie still leaned over, looking under the bushes. "That is approximately where Izzy saw him trimming and raking last night about this time."

"Him?" The deputy pounced on the word.

"The gardener, José. It did not seem like a normal time to garden. At first, we thought he did so after the pool area closed to keep from disturbing the guests. Or perhaps once the sun went down because the temperature is cooler. I told Sheriff Tate all of this."

"Uh, huh." He turned back toward the pool

and canteen area with his back toward them. "Does seem rather weird." He slipped the evidence bag into a pocket of his coat. "I'll get this to the lab, but first I want to speak to this José fella."

Connie reached for her phone. "I'll call the Blakelys." She moved to the Canteen area nearer to the building where there was better light—if the glow from the soda machine could be called that—and sat down.

"Good." He slowed and turned back toward the bushes like he was going to stand guard. "Tell them to bring him here."

A minute later, Connie hung up. "Mr. Blakely will bring the gardener here. He lives in the bunkhouse."

The man nodded "Thank you, ladies. You can leave now. Have a good night."

Connie's mouth dropped wide open, then she shut it. With a small shrug to Elizabeth and Izzy across the pool, she rose with a scrape of the chair and walked off in the direction of her cabin.

Elizabeth followed, her steps shuffling in her bedroom slippers to catch up.

Izzy hung behind.

The deputy turned his gaze from watching the two ladies retreat to their cabin. "Yes? You had somethin' else?"

She did, but should she reveal it to him? "If I discuss it with you now, they might get suspicious." Her eyes shifted to the retreating women and back to the deputy.

"You think one of them might be involved?"

She gulped. "No, but with all that has happened . . ."

He gave a slow nod. "I understand. You don't want to be pegged as the one pointing the finger."

Something like that. Izzy lowered her gaze.

"Okay." The deputy pushed off the tree trunk and turned away from her. "Guard this area while I get some tape out of my car to cordon it off. Then I'll take your statement."

She watched as he strode off, then sat at one of the tables. Connie and Elizabeth had gone inside their cabin. Izzy sat alone in the darkened area, with only the muffed rumbles of distant thunder accompanying the ripples lapping at the edges of the pool tiles. Probably less than two minutes had passed since he left, though it seemed like a half-hour.

She tried to unjumble the thoughts that tapped through her brain. Something didn't jive. Why would a gardener poison a well-known, high-profile attorney?

Who did he cover up for? Bob Blakely was Ramona's godfather. Could that be the connection? Had he found the vial and buried it to avoid any suspicion falling on his employer? Mrs. Blakely had brought Vernon Roberts his tea.

Her head ached. "You aren't cut out for this. Leave it to the experts." She whispered the reprimand to her reflection in the pool as she heard the telltale footsteps of cowboy boots approaching.

Before she could turn around, a large hand covered her mouth, and a strong arm yanked her from the chair, dragging her into the darkness.

Chapter Sixteen

Nabbed

"Don't say a word. Come with me, and I won't hurt you." The male voice hissed the command into Izzy's ear. His breath smelled of garlic. His clothes held a slight odor of sweat and horse dung.

She nodded and squeezed her eyes shut. *Lord, help me.*

He dragged her behind the Canteen and then across a short field to a wooden shed. "Inside." He released his hand from her face and shoved her in the back. "And don't scream. I do have a gun."

Izzy tumbled to the ground. Something sharp, like a piece of wood, dug into her palm as she braced her fall. "Ay."

"I said—"

"Okay. Okay." She sucked at the wound on her hand and scooted upright into a sitting position.

The face remained hidden in the dark, even with the door open. In fact, the whole man stood silhouetted against the white flashes that outlined the billowing black clouds to the west. The wind whooshed through the shed and tussled his hair. Had to be José. It couldn't be bald Mr. Blakely.

A silvery flash lit up the small storage room then the vibrations from the billowing cloud pressure jostled it. The wooden structure creaked and moaned in response.

"The deputy told me to stay put. When he returns and sees me gone, he will start looking."

The man took two steps inside the shed. "Then I guess I better hide ya."

Well, that didn't go as Izzy had planned. Perhaps she should have kept her mouth shut.

He took off his belt and she cowered, half expecting him to strike her with it the way her father had whipped her for punishment as a small child. All those long-ago emotions raced into her throat.

Instead, he pulled her to her feet then wrapped the belt around her arms and torso. As he yanked the leather tighter, it cut into her skin. She whimpered, more in fear than pain.

"Sorry." Locking her under his arm, he shoved her face near his armpit. The pungent sourness of his body odor made her gag more than the dusty rag he shoved into her mouth. Then her nose detected something else. Aftershave. Musky, like the deputy's.

Her eyes had become more adjusted to the darkness. She glanced down to his feet. Cowboy boots. Dark pants. Something hard on his waist jabbed her ribs. A flashlight? A gun?

Oh no. It was the deputy!

Mumbling a scream, she tried to wiggle free as he grabbed a roll of duct tape and tore off a piece with his teeth. He slapped it over the bit of rag in her mouth, then applied another strip to the belt around her wrists. When she struggled, he seized her by the shoulders and shook her angrily.

"Shut up! I told you, I won't hurt you. But you better behave." He shoved her to the floor. Then he jerked her legs up and wrapped the duct tape around her ankles and again around her knees.

Every muscle in her body ached, especially in her shoulder blades. What would he do with her?

He crouched down and peered into her face. In the dim light, his face looked a little different, but familiar. Awfully familiar. The gardener! She inhaled sharply. The deputy was José?

He must have noticed the recognition on her face. His lips twisted into a sinister grin. "So, you figured it out, huh? Smart woman." He jerked the badge off his Khaki shirt and tossed it to the ground. "Kid's badge. Hand them out at the rodeos like candy."

His face inched toward hers and the garlic smell rushed into her nose again, making her cringe. "Easy enough to fake looking like a sheriff's deputy in the dark. Especially since I heard the sheriff over your friend's speaker phone telling you he'd be sending someone."

He stood and hauled her to her feet. "I came around the back of the Canteen, fully expecting to dig up the bottle and toss it in the creek. But there you two sat. You nosy witches had found it first." He scooted her backward to the wall of the shed.

"Stay here while I saddle a horse."

A horse? Where would he take her? She mumbled a scream again.

He laughed and closed the door.

The sound of a lock clicking echoed in Izzy's ears. Then stillness. Except the rumbling thunder growing closer. Izzy felt a cold shudder ripple through her body. How could she have been so stupid?

Wait. A spark of hope flittered in her mind. The sheriff would still send someone. Then Connie and Elizabeth would notice Izzy hadn't gone back to her cabin. They'd all begin to search for her.

Surely José had thought of that, though. He had to have a plan. Probably to kill her and dispose of her body. She'd always figured she'd rejoice when the Lord called her home, but now the possibility twisted her gut. *Not yet, please. I'm too young.* Her son and his wife were expecting their first in four months. She wanted to see her grandchild born.

Despair washed over her as she stood braced against the wall in the blackness. She tried to grasp verses from the Psalms about God's protection, but none of them floated to her conscience. The building shook from more thunder and white blasts shot through the slits in the walls.

Where are you, Lord? Please send Connie to find me. She knows your voice. She'd listen. She'd come.

A blinding white streak hit her face. Izzy squinted. It took her brain a moment to register what happened. A flash of lightning struck as José opened the shed door. Her eyes began to refocus on his silhouette. He yanked her toward him and then lifted her over his shoulder like a sack of potatoes.

Izzy wiggled, screamed as loud as she could under the gag, and pounded her tied fists against his back, but to no avail. She pressed her knees into his ribs over and over, yet he did not flinch. He only kept walking. She pressed in harder and tried to kick her feet.

José stopped. "Enough, woman." With one swoop he unloaded her onto the ground.

Flat on her back, she lost her breath for a

moment, but could barely cough through the gag. Stunned, she winced as a rock scraped across her back. The man dragged her by her feet to his horse. She curled her upper body to her face, reached up and pulled the tape off of part of her face. She was only able to get an edge free before he lifted her and flopped her onto her stomach over the neck of his horse.

Again, she lost her breath, but clung to a section of the saddle. The western horn dug into her side, and she clawed at the hair of the animal to keep her from toppling forward. At this point, holding on took both of her hands.

With a hand pressed on her rear end, her captor swung himself into the saddle. The leather creaked and moaned under his weight. He clicked his teeth, and the horse began to trot, then cantor. Izzy turned her head, trying to peer beyond the mane to see where they headed. Each thud of the hooves vibrated across her jaw as her face jammed into the animal's muscles. The fur coat scraped across her bouncing cheek.

The thunder and lightning grew closer in sync and illuminated the plains. Flash-rumble, Flashboom. As they headed down a slope, hard icy drops pounded her back. First a few, then more. The smell of wet fur and leather mingled in her nostrils.

The horse lost its footing, briefly, as they slid down a hill, then righted itself. Then Izzy saw the creek. The dark water churned and bubbled as the rain pounded it. She reached up and tugged on the gag again, loosening one edge enough to pull the rag out of her mouth.

José jerked Izzy by the arms and half-dragged, half-carried her to the edge. "Have a nice swim. The floods around here happen fast and furious. By the time they find you, you'll be well downstream. And if this rain keeps up, they might find your friend right alongside you." He shoved her into the raging swells.

"No!" She screamed but this time the sound was muted by a mouth full of muddy water. She sputtered and coughed, then she ripped the rest of the tape from her mouth and took a deep breath of air. The water wrapped around her in a ka-woosh, then rose, and fell as the waves blanketed her. Her head hit something hard and sharp. The sting zapped through her skull.

Izzy struggled to keep her head out of the creek. Water lapped into her ears. The rain pounded into her eyes. A chill shuddered through her as her clothing weighed her down. All her senses sharpened to the flashes of light, the sloughing of the current and the drumming of the rain. Her feet hit the ground and she shoved herself upward. Somewhere, she'd heard to point her feet downstream. Her limbs numbed to the cold as she bobbed under the weight of the restraints. Her neck ached from being strained to keep her face above the water as it billowed around her.

Lord, save me. Mees Fanny, she needs me, Lord. You know she depends upon me. Please, for her sake. She is Your servant, Lord.

Her silent prayer rambled as her tears mixed with the raindrops and became swallowed in the stream.

Then a crack split the night and vibrated in her submerged ears. Lightning struck a mesquite tree on the other side.

A huge limb groaned then fell into the creek with a huge ker-splash. For a moment, she was lost in the wave it caused, but it slowed the water as it settled into the torrent and halted her forward motion for a brief moment.

God heard her pleas. He sent her a tree branch.

She would live.

Thank You, God.

She took in the deepest breath she could manage, held it, and rolled to the side. With her legs tied together, Izzy dolphin-kicked toward the bobbing wood and reached as far as her fingers could stretch for a branch as it floated by her. Thank goodness the water had stretched the leather enough for her to move her arms a bit.

Success. The limb turned and bumped next to her hip. Scrambling, she pulled herself onto it and clung to it as best she could with her toes curled around the wood and her hips pressed into the bark. She used her forearms to squeeze the sides of the limb and breathed long, lung-filling breaths through her nose.

The thorns from the wispy-leaved branches scraped her face, but she didn't care. She clung to the long branch and concentrated on breathing. The rising water splashed across her face, burned her nostrils, and threatened to fill her lungs.

A rushing sound grew. She raised her face to see jagged river rocks peeking out of the waves. The water swirled and foamed over them. Izzy braced for impact.

Thud. The broken end of the branch hit the first boulder and almost shook Izzy loose. She found her footing and gave a mighty jump toward the bank. She released the branch as it bolted into the center of the stream and down a treacherous, rocky hill. Again, she hit the bottom, several feet closer to the bank. She pushed against it with everything she had and landed on the edge of a grassy inlet. She lifted her torso onto the side of the sloped bank. With a thorny bush to use as an anchor, she pulled herself out of the swirls and scooted in inch-worm action until her feet left the water.

Her chest heaved from exhaustion as she rolled over onto her back, staring into the rain pounding her cheeks. Still, she was too close to the flood to be comfortable. She shoved herself up the slight hill until she lay a few yards from the wash. Then she breathed deeply. New tears streamed down her cheeks. She sent up another prayer of thanks as a nervous laugh bubbled through her swollen lips.

The gurgling of the rushing creek rolled through her consciousness as white noise. The cold dampness still seeped all the way to her bones keeping her shoulders in a constant state of shiver, but the thunder rumbled less loudly, and the flashes of lightning had passed. The rain dwindled to a soft dripping, then stopped altogether as weariness consumed her. Her head pounded, but after a while her mind could no longer register it. She gave in and let all her muscles go limp.

Izzy closed her eyes, and an unusually warm peace cloaked her. Then the world became pitch black and void of sound.

Chapter Seventeen

Rescue

"Izzy. Izzy!" Connie's voice filtered into her dream as a distant echo.

Whiteness surrounded her. Her eyes felt as if someone had sewn them shut. Her head ached a thousand times more than it ever had in her life. Moving even one neck muscle made it worse.

"Izzy. Can you hear me?"

I can, but my mouth won't respond. Let me sleep. Go away.

A hand shook her gently. Someone jiggled her legs and the tape screeched. The sting from its release around her ankles hurt almost as much as her aching muscles. The belt released its leathery grip. Suddenly, her hands dropped to her side, hitting the wet earth beside her resting place. The sudden action sent icy hot pain through her shoulders.

She moaned.

Slowly she forced her eyes to open, then squeezed her lids shut to keep the bright light from invading. *What in the world?*

"She's coming around."

Connie's voice? For real? I'm found?

She heard the crackle of tires on gravel. The rush of the creek, less of a roar than before. The squeak, squeak, squeak of wheels. Men's footsteps.

"Ma'am? Ma'am. Can you hear me?" A male voice. A warm hand rested on her shoulder. "Are you hurt any place?"

"Every place." It croaked off her tongue in a raspy sound. She scrunched her forehead. "My head. It's pounding."

She heard a screech of velcro then cloth wrapping around her arm. The pressure began to pump tighter. Blood pressure cuff. A finger lifted her eye lid and flashed a bright light into it. Now her head really hurt in front and back.

"BP 110 over 52. Pupils slightly responsive, right more than left. Pulse low, body temperature 95.2. Hypothermia possible."

Hands lifted her from the damp ground and onto a dry pallet. Maybe a gurney. A warm blanket was swaddled around her, and an oxygen mask placed over her nose and mouth.

"Breathe normally. You're going to be fine." A soothing male voice filtered into her consciousness.

The pallet raised upward and started to move. The forward motions over the uneven ground jerked her from side to side. It hurt but not as much as the horse ride. They must have been wheeling her over a bumpy field. Izzy squinted and saw Connie's face as she jogged alongside her. It took all of Izzy's strength just to lift her arm and reach for the woman.

"I'm here, Izzy. You're going to be okay."

Another jerk, then a bump. They shoved the gurney headfirst inside a vehicle. Thunking of shoes sounded and then the shuffling of feet. Someone gently turned her arm, so her hand faced upward. "Starting the IV. You'll feel a pinch, ma'am. Try not to flinch."

A cold wet something rubbed her forearm near her elbow then the needle jabbed her skin. Izzy squeaked, but the sting subsided.

The blood pressure cuff whirred and crunched her bicep again. She wanted to scream for them to leave her alone, to stop. *Please, I just want to sleep.* But common sense told her to remain quiet. Their actions were to help her, not harm her.

Connie grabbed her hand, her soft fingers gripping hers. "I'm right here, Izzy. They're taking you to the hospital. The worst is over."

Izzy heard the engine rev up and the vehicle lurched. The wheels wobbled over the rough turf for a moment but finally hummed rhythmically over a solid surface.

An EMT hovered over her, monitoring her vitals, and murmuring to his partners. Then his hand touched her arm and softly squeezed it. "Hang in there, Izzy. We have a bit of a ride into Kerrville. Just relax. You're doing great."

"No sirens?" Her voice squeaked.

He patted her arm again. "That's a good thing. You aren't in that much danger. But they're using the flashers."

That made her smile. "Never been in an ambulance."

He dabbed her lips with a lemony tartness that made her mouth water. It felt good to swallow through the sandpaper feeling in her throat.

"Does that help the dryness in your mouth? Can't give you water until they examine you, but you're getting plenty through the I.V."

"Had enough water for a while." Izzy tried to laugh, but it made her throat hurt more. It came out in a series of coughs.

The EMT and Connie both chuckled.

"Yes, ma'am. I imagine you have." The kind man smiled down at her.

"So . . . tired . . ." Izzy closed her eyes to everything and plunged back into the blackness.

The sound of voices and beeping of a machine floated Izzy out of her dream state. Her body felt dry, warm, and pain-free. Soft sheets, smelling faintly of bleach, enveloped her skin. She groaned and struggled to open her eyes, but the light made her squint again and her eyelids still felt weighted.

Slowly, Connie's face came into focus. Then Miss Fanny's.

"There you are, my dear." Miss Fanny smiled down at her.

"I'll get the nurse." Connie let go of Izzy's hand, and her footsteps receded.

"I'm in the hospital?"

"Yes, dear. You have a slight concussion and some mild hypothermia, but you are going to be right as rain." Miss Fanny's hand flew to her mouth. "Oops. Wrong choice of words."

Izzy grinned but it made her head hurt. She had been rescued. Not a dream. Safe and sound. "He saved me."

"Who, dear?"

"God. I was about to drown, and lightning hit a tree. The limb crashed into the water. I clung to it."

Miss Fanny's warm hand folded around hers. "Noah had an ark. He sent a whale to Jonah. Paul clung to debris in a shipwreck. So why not?"

The elderly woman bowed her head and began

to whisper. Izzy barely heard an "amen" before she drifted back to the still blackness once again. But this time it came with a deep peace.

Chapter Eighteen

Storm Passed

The third time she woke, the fuzziness in Izzy's brain and the pain in her head faded more quickly when the light hit her eyes.

She turned to see Connie curled into a chair, almost in a fetal position. Her hair hung loosely from her normal bun and half-masked her face. Izzy sighed and gazed out the window. Fluffy blue clouds hung in an azure sky. She wondered what floor her room sat on. Outside her slightly opened door, the bustling nursing staff shuffled and chatted in the halls. The aroma of chicken whiffed into her nostrils, making her stomach gurgle. The soft rhythmic beeps of her monitor almost lulled her back to nether land, but she resisted.

Connie stirred and then her green eyes flew open. "Oh, you're awake." She stretched her long legs out of their curled position and shoved the strands of hair behind one ear. "How are you feeling?"

"Better. I smell food."

Laughter floated over her. "Then you are better. Let me get your nurse."

She left, and Izzy gazed out the window again. The storm had passed. In more ways than one.

After taking her vitals, and fussing a bit with her I.V., the nurse brought Izzy some chicken broth and lime gelatin. Never had anything so tasty slid down her throat.

Connie sat perched on the side of her bed, ready to assist her if needed. She poured some cool water into a paper cup and bent a plastic straw before popping it into the cup. "Here you go. Not too much too fast, now."

Izzy finished her meal and then leaned back into the pillows. "How did you find me?"

"The sheriff's deputy was on the way to the ranch. He had to circle around the low water crossing and come up on the other side across the fields once the water began to rise. He noticed you lying there. You weren't responsive." The muscles in her neck wobbled. "He called the EMTs and then the sheriff. The sheriff called me. Aunt Fanny wanted to rush to your aid, but the rain hadn't stopped. I persuaded her to stay at the ranch, and I came out in the jeep with Mr. Blakely."

"José?"

"Arrested. When neither he nor you could be found, it became pretty obvious what had happened. Especially when I described the first deputy . . ." She lifted her fingers into quotation signs. ". . . to Sheriff Tate. It wasn't anyone he knew."

She moved back to her chair and sat. "I ran outside and saw no police cruiser. The Blakelys found me by the pool and said José wasn't in the bunkhouse after all. You weren't in your room. That's when the apparent answer hit me. José had pretended to be a deputy, taken the vial, and kidnapped you."

"He saw us dig up the vial and heard you call the sheriff." The man had admitted that much.

Connie nodded. "As soon as the worst of the storm lifted, the Blakelys and the sheriff organized a manhunt. On horseback, José got fairly far, but the storm hindered him as well. They found him in one of the limestone caves on the far end of the ranch. He's here, too, by the way."

"In the hospital?"

"Seems he ruptured his spleen from a broken rib. Had a lot of bruising, too. Any idea why?"

Izzy lifted her chin as realization dawned on her. "I pounded him with my tied-up fists and knees when he carried me over his shoulder to the horse. I guess I am stronger than I thought."

"Guess so." Connie smiled at her.

Fear hit Izzy's brain. "He cannot get to me, can he?" The door squeaked open. She flinched and stiffened.

Connie rose. "Don't worry, Izzy. He's well-guarded."

Sheriff Tate stepped in. When he saw her awake and alert, he looked relieved. "Well, you look better."

Izzy smiled. "Hi, Sheriff. I understand your deputy found me. Thank him for me, will you?"

He pulled up another chair and sat beside her. "Sure 'nuff. Feel like talking?"

"Sí." She gave a slight bob of her head.

"Tell me what happened." He took out his ever-present notebook and pen. This time, he also pulled out his phone. "Mind if I record this?"

"Not at all." She explained about the kidnapping and José impersonating the deputy while the sheriff scratched notes on his pad.

Connie shook her head. "He seemed so legit."

Sheriff Tate eyed her. "We're still looking into his background."

Izzy eased up onto the pillow. "Did he poison Vernon Roberts?" It still seemed so surreal to her.

Connie nodded. "It appears so."

"But, why?" Her eyes darted back and forth between the sheriff and her employer's niece.

"José Mendoza was born in Houston as Joseph Meadows. His mother was Hispanic and his father Anglo. Mendoza was her maiden name."

"Mendoza? Wait. His paintings are for sale in the lobby of the Circle C." Izzy blinked. "And for quite a good amount of money."

"Very observant, Mrs. Gutierrez." The sheriff

sat back and hitched his foot onto his knee. "Seems he had a gardening business as well as being an artist on the side. Vernon Roberts hired him to do his lawns, and he worked there for several years. Roberts said he was good at the landscaping, and he even hired his wife as a housekeeper. Then one weekend, Roberts came home unexpectedly from a business trip and found the two of them using his house for a party. He fired them both."

"Well, of course. Anyone would do the same." Connie crossed her arms.

"Yes, but Roberts went on to say that he made sure no one in Houston would hire them again. From there it's a little sketchy. José isn't talking, but we found a record of his wife's death only a few months after they were fired. The EMTs found her at the bottom of the stairs at their apartment. Apparently, he was with a friend on the other side of town. The death was listed as suspicious, but with no evidence and no witnesses, no charges could be made."

"What?" Izzy's jaw dropped.

Connie rolled her eyes. "Yeah. Exactly my reaction."

"You think he might have killed her?"

"Or maybe she killed herself. Either way, I think he somehow blamed Roberts for it. But that's just guessing." The sheriff shrugged. "Like I said, José isn't talking. But he left Houston right after that, changed his name, and got odd jobs here and there over the next few years. Finally, he ended up on the Blakely ranch and had worked there for going on two years now. Solid employee, never had any trouble according to them." The sheriff shook his head. "Guess when he watched Roberts get off the bus, something snapped inside."

Izzy inched up in the bed a bit more. "It is a little hard to believe that he was so upstanding. He did not seem to have a single concern about tossing me into the swollen stream to die."

"I don't have any answers for you about that, but it does make me wonder about his wife's death. And I just bet that Roberts's survival was a complete accident." The sheriff ran his hands through his hair.

"But you don't know that for sure." Connie offered the cup to Izzy for another sip of water.

"He isn't saying, upon advice of his attorney.

He does admit he got the idea from talking with Ramona Redding, though." He rose and twisted his Stetson in his hands. "I will need your formal statement if you don't mind. I can get it off this recording, but it will require your signature. I'll get it typed up and bring it back in the morning, okay?" He patted his phone and put it in his pocket. Then he turned to Connie.

"Ladies, I owe you both an apology. Especially you, Miss Wright. I shouldn't have jumped down your throat about that bottle."

Connie raised her chin. "Thank you. But it all worked out. No hard feelings."

He gave her an ever so slight bow. "No, ma'am. You two actually helped us a good deal." He laughed. "Seems a whole bunch of folks didn't care for the man, did they?"

With that he placed his hat back on his head and exited.

Connie adjusted the pillows behind Izzy's back. "I honestly can't blame them. Vernon Roberts definitely needs prayer, doesn't he? Perhaps this incident will be a wake-up call for him."

Izzy shrugged. "You never know. God can do amazing things." Last night proved that. "And He can use terrible things for good."

"Yes, He can. Speaking of good. The fundraiser went amazingly well. Janice is being vetted and if all works out, I plan to make her our Midwest liaison. She could use a change of scenery. Her father has already made a sizeable donation to Equine Engage's new location. In fact, they are naming the stables after him."

"Wow."

"And, totaling up the rest that came in this past weekend, the Sanderson's have almost two-thirds of the funds needed to open next year."

Izzy clapped her bandaged hands. "Connie, that is amazing."

Connie grinned. "I actually think the events of the weekend made them open their pockets a bit wider."

Izzy nodded. "And for me as well. I have a small CD coming due. I would like to make a larger donation, too. In thanksgiving."

"That's wonderful." Connie placed her hand to her heart "Truly. Thank you. It means so much."

"When can I get out of here?"

"Maybe tomorrow? But don't worry. The Blakelys are spoiling Aunt Fanny. She even went horseback riding again yesterday. And she told me to tell you she doesn't expect you back on duty for at least a week if not more."

"But . . ."

"No buts about it. You deserve a bit of pampering, dear lady." Connie wagged her finger playfully as her smile increased. "Besides, I plan to stay until you are fully recovered so I can help out. I have a bit of a lull until the next fundraiser anyway and I'd love to spend time with my favorite aunt." Connie reached into a canvas bag. "Oh, and Mrs. Blakely had your clothes laundered. All the mud and slime came out just fine."

"Great. I'll be glad to get out of this hospital gown."

Connie moved to open a door to show some hanging clothes. "She packed your gown and robe, too. And toothbrush and hairbrush."

Izzy laced her hands together. "Bless her."

"Okay." She pulled the shirt that Izzy had been wearing the day before out of the wardrobe. "I have been meaning to ask you." Connie chuckled and held up Izzy's t-shirt against her chest. "What's this mean?"

"Binge Jesus?" Izzy pushed up on her elbows. "That is about watching *The Chosen*, the streaming show about the disciples of Christ. It is one of my favorites."

Connie tucked the shirt back into the wardrobe. "I've heard of that. Maybe I can take an evening off and do a little binging of my own."

"You would enjoy it, I think." Izzy paused. With her new friend taking such good care of her, her conscience pinged. More like rattled loudly through her. "I have a confession to make. For a brief time, I actually wondered about your involvement in Mr. Roberts's poisoning." She put her hands in front of her. "Only because you are such a powerful businesswoman and are so passionate about your causes."

Connie scrunched her forehead. "I guess that's almost a compliment. But I don't blame you, Izzy. To be honest, I briefly wondered about you as well. In fact, about the only person I didn't suspect was Aunt—"

"Fanny." Izzy finished her sentence in laughter. "Me, too."

"Did someone call my name?"

The two turned to see a stately elderly lady push a rollator into the room. In the well under its flip-up bench sat a vase with a huge bouquet of flowers. "You need a room brightener."

Connie lifted the vase out.

"Thank you, Mees Fanny." The arrangement was beautiful with stargazer lilies. Her favorite.

The three admired the spring arrangement as Connie set it on Izzy's bedside table. As soon as she did, a ray of sunlight streamed in and illuminated each petal in brilliance.

Izzy smiled as Miss Fanny moved to the bed and took her hand. Connie came to grasp the other one, and her new friend lifted up thanks to the Almighty for His amazing display of provision, protection, and love.

The Visitor **Meets Old Hairy**

Preview by Fay Lamb

For about the fifth time, Polly had to turn to her sister with her finger to her lips.

In the darkness, it was a little hard to see, but slowly, Polly's eyes were becoming accustomed to her surroundings.

"I'm not talking." Connie's attempt to whisper had the decibels of a seven-forty-seven. "I'm walking here." Wind whipped hair into her face. "And who can hear anything with this wind." She swirled her hands above her head to indicate the swishing leaves. "Give us a little rain, and we'll have a hurricane."

"Try not to step on the twigs." Polly ignored her sister's complaints.

"We're not on a path, Polly. The ground is littered with them."

Ethan's snicker took the air of frustration from Polly's wings. She leaned against a tree and covered her face with her hands, trying to keep from bursting into laughter.

Connie leaned against her, her body shaking. "And if Old Hairy was out here, we most definitely would see him."

"No." Ethan came near. "Aunt Connie, you're not up on your Bigfoot information. They're stealthy. They are hard to spot even in the daytime. They can hide themselves against the trees and not make a sound unless they want to be heard or seen—all eight feet—no grunting from exertion, no stomping when they walk." He glanced at his mom with a sly smile that barely showed in the moonlight. "Some people even believe they have a cloaking ability like one of those lizards in Florida that change colors."

Marc drew near. "And they can read your mind." He wiggled his brows and glanced at his wife. "When they're near you, their sub-sonic hum can make you deathly ill."

They were making fun of her, but Polly didn't care. Standing alone with her family in the middle of their expedition area and gabbing with the people she loved, that was all she wanted. "They hide in caves and traverse that way. That's why they aren't seen," she countered with her own knowledge of Bigfoot lore. "And they've had years to adapt to the land, and they know the layout."

"There are no caves in this park." Ethan swatted at a mosquito that by some show of strength moved against the wind.

They remained silent for a moment as the limbs above them rustled.

"Did you hear that?" Connie spun around.

"With the wind?" Polly threw her sister's words back at her.

Connie waved her hands back and forth in front of her face. "And smell that?"

Polly took a deep breath and coughed. "That's not a Bigfoot." The wind must have brought the odor to them.

"It's a skunk." Ethan took off running through the dark in the direction of the camp.

Connie put her hands out to stop Marc and Polly. "Let's see if he runs into it first."

Marc laughed aloud. "Good idea."

Polly spied something illuminated by the rays of the moon filtering through the trees—the white of a skunk's coat.

Perhaps Ethan had been the clever one.

Polly held to her sister's and her husband's arms. "There." She nodded.

The skunk stood up on two feet and looked around.

Polly held her breath, and not from the stench. Did skunks attack?

The skunk stayed still for a moment, looked behind it, and then turned to look in their direction.

Polly planted her feet so as to run if it moved toward her.

"Did it widen its eyes?" Marc joked.

Despite the wind, tromping on the grass could be heard and then came a heavy grunt.

The skunk took off.

Connie—and Marc—jumped behind Polly's back.

More stomping sounded, coming closer.

An overly large figure silhouetted in the moon's shine moved into the center of the trees. His attention was in the direction the skunk had fled.

Connie gasped.

The creature stilled completely. Then it turned.

"Stay still." Marc's whisper was a command. "Polly, is it a man?"

"I-I don't think so." She trembled. "He's huge."

The huge apelike man stared. When it blinked, the action was slow.

It swayed back and forth like an ape.

"We're about to find out if it's color blind." Polly reached for her sister's hand.

Connie held on to her. "Not funny, Pollyanna."

"Wasn't trying to be." Polly took a step back, forcing Marc and Connie to come with her.

The creature blinked again. Then it raised its shoulders, bent low at the knees, and inhaled. As it stood again, a tremendous howl built from its innards and reverberated against Polly. She'd never heard anything the likes of it.

The howl ended, and the creature stood stock-still, his attention never leaving them.

"Shoo. Shoo." Connie moved her free hand.

The lumbering beast stared at Connie, blinked again, and turned. Then it thundered off into the woods.

Polly released her breath. "Was it really . . ."

Enjoy The Visitors Next Trip

Scan QR code for a direct link for purchase.

From the Story
Original King Ranch Chicken
circa 1948

Ingredients

1 (10 3/4 ounce) can cream of chicken soup
1 (10 3/4 ounce) can cream of mushroom soup
1 (10 ounce) can Ro-tel diced tomatoes (with green chilies)
1 cup chicken broth (or more, to taste)
1/2 cup chopped onion
1/2 cup chopped green pepper
16 ounces Monterey jack cheese
1 whole chicken cooked, deboned, then shredded
12 corn tortillas

Directions

1. Boil chicken, remove meat from skin and bones. (Save broth). Shred it by using two forks and pulling the meat apart in small pieces. (You can use 6-8 chicken breasts instead of a whole chicken.)

3. Finely chop and sauté onions and green pepper.

4. Mix with soups, Ro-tel, shredded chicken, and chicken broth.

5. Line bottom of Pyrex casserole with six corn tortillas.

6. Add 1/2 of chicken/soup mixture; spread over tortillas. Sprinkle grated cheese over mixture.

7. Then make another layer of six tortillas, chicken/soup mixture, and cheese.

8. Cover with foil and bake at 250-300 F for one hour until cheese is bubbly.

Serves 8-10

Add sliced black olives and a dollop of sour cream on top of each serving if desired.

Counter Point by Marji Laine

Her father's gone. Her diner's closing. Her car's in the lake. Cat McPherson has nothing left to lose. Except for her life. And a madman's bent on taking that away.

Her former boyfriend, Ray Alexander, returns as a hero from his foreign mission with a fallen cartel king on his tail. The man threatens all the people that Ray loves. So why are several attempts made on Cat's life? Loved or not, she must learn to trust Ray, the man who broke her heart.

Keeping Cat safe from this powerful man might prove impossible for Ray, but after seeing his mission destroyed, he knows better than to ignore the man's threats. Cat's resistance to his protection and the stirring of his long-denied feelings for her complicate his intentions, placing them both in a fight for their lives.

Acknowledgments

Thank you for reading The Visitor Makes a Retreat. I hope you enjoyed it.

Fifteen years ago, as a freelance reporter for a local magazine, I was assigned an article about equine therapy. I had never heard of this form of assistance for the mentally and physically challenged, so the topic intrigued me. I visited several of these stables in and around Fort Worth and became immediately impressed by the dedication of the trainers and volunteers. I witnessed children with severe disabilities smiling and laughing, brushing down the animals and feeding them. Others joyously swept and mucked the stables. I saw worth shining in these children and teenagers' eyes, and hope swelling in their countenances.

That experience became branded in my heart, and I want to thank Write Integrity Press for allowing me the opportunity to include such a worthwhile endeavor in my novella. If you ever have the opportunity to visit one of these stables, I highly encourage it. So many have sprung up throughout the United States. I am confident each is doing amazing work and is worth supporting.

Thanks to all of the amazing writers who have joined together to make The Visitor series, and especially to those who edited it and who proofread it. I am honored to have my mystery be the first in the series and thank the editor in chief, Marji Laine, for selecting it.

And above all, I give glory to my Lord who has graced me with combining my two loves, writing and cozy mysteries, which allowed me to weave this story together.

Julie Cosgrove

About Julie B Cosgrove

Whodunnit? My mom used to ask us that with a hand cocked on her hip, peering into our wide-eyed faces. Naturally the blame trickled down to the youngest one—me. I had to solve the crime so I could plead my innocence.

On walks through the Texas Hill Country with my dad, I became a keen observer of nature, and later in life as an adult and writer, of human nature. So sleuthing is part of my DNA.

I wrote award-winning works in high school creative writing class, but then life edged in. Even so, on my long commutes I'd make up storylines in my head. After my husband passed away, the desire to write returned. My sister suggested I write mysteries, which had long been my favorite genre.

Now I absorb mysteries whenever I get the chance then let the whodunnits capture my imagination, and my keyboard. I think I'm finally becoming who God intend me to be.

Besides writing mystery, suspense-romance, and short stories, I am a freelance editor. For the past ten years, I have regularly written for several devotional publications, and recently retired from being a content editor for CRU Canada's devotionals. My own blog, *Where Did You Find God Today*, has readers in over 50 countries. Preview my works, blog, and editorial prices on my website at www.juliebcosgrove.com

Julie B Cosgrove

Also By Julie
Relatively Seeking Mysteries

Genealogy searches uncover more than simple ancestry in these three stories. With each layer of historical revelation, others get nervous. Enough to threaten the three young ladies who have mastered the skills of research.

Wordplay Mysteries

Wanda Warner and her friends are avid wordplay enthusiasts, from Scrabble and Boggle to crosswords and word-finds. True mystery-buffs, they also have a tendency to snoop, sometimes poking their noses into places they don't belong and stirring up issues that shouldn't be stirred. Between keeping themselves safe from real trouble and keeping the local police and their

neighbors from fussing, they have their hands full in these mystery novels.

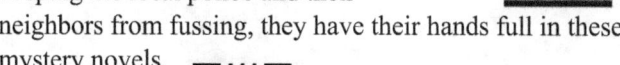

Thank you
for reading our books!

Please consider leaving a review for the author
on the purchase page for this book.

Look for other books
published by

P

Pursued Books
an imprint of

W

Write Integrity Press
www.WriteIntegrity.com

www.ingramcontent.com/pod-product-compliance
Lightning Source LLC
Chambersburg PA
CBHW072234170626
46813CB00003B/1224